Work What You Got

Also by Stephanie Perry Moore

Prime Choice
Pressing Hard
Problem Solved
Prayed Up
Promise Kept

Work What You Got

A Beta Gamma Pi Novel
Book 1

Stephanie Perry Moore

KENSINGTON PUBLISHING CORP.

www.kensingtonbooks.com

DAFINA BOOKS are published by

Kensington Publishing Corp.
850 Third Avenue
New York, NY 10022

All Kensington titles, imprints, and distributed lines are available at special quantity discounts for bulk purchases for sales promotion, premiums, fund-raising, educational, or institutional use.

Special book excerpts or customized printings can also be created to fit specific needs. For details, write or phone the office of the Kensington Special Sales Manager: Attn. Special Sales Department. Kensington Publishing Corp., 850 Third Avenue, New York, NY 10022. Phone: 1-800-221-2647.

Dafina and the Dafina logo Reg. U.S. Pat. & TM Off.

ISBN-13: 978-0-7582-2542-9
ISBN-10: 0-7582-2542-3

First Printing: January 2009
10 9 8 7 6 5 4 3 2 1

Printed in the United States of America

For
Dr. Yvonne Kennedy,
Marcia L. Fudge, Esq.,
and Gwendolyn E. Boyd
(past presidents of my beloved sorority)

Know that the legacy of your leadership
inspires me daily to work it like you did!
I pray that together we'll keep on
making this world a better place.
And that every reader will understand the importance
of giving all they've got to help someone else.

ACKNOWLEDGMENTS

Sorority life is something I know a thing or two about. I've been a member of Delta Sigma Theta Sorority, Inc., since the fall of 1989. I can say my pledge experience was a lot. Honestly, I got my feelings hurt and I hurt some folks' feelings. Thankfully, we stuck it out and all was good. However, even as an adult, I know being in a sorority takes a lot of work. But I've found that when the heart is right, the bond is deep. To be a member of a sorority you have to be ready to care about others as much as you care about yourself. If followed, this simple biblical principle can make the bond of sisterhood a rewarding experience.

Penning a novel on leadership in a sorority makes me dig even deeper into my own soul. I firmly believe that any organization is only as strong as its leaders. It's not about getting your way or being popular, it is about helping your group know that only together can they make the world a better place. There is a leader inside us all, and I pray you seek God to help make you a great one. Here is a big thank you to all who show me different leadership qualities that help me soar in my writing world.

To my family, parents, Dr. Franklin and Shirley Perry, Sr.; brother, Dennis, and sister-in-law, Leslie; my mother-in-law, Ms. Ann; and to my extended family, Reverend Walter and Marjorie Kimbrough, Bobby and Sarah Lundy, Antonio and Gloria London, Cedric and Nicole Smith, Harry and Nino Colon, and Brett and Loni Perriman, what *strength* you show me. It's not easy to tell inspiring stories, but you always lift me up. I'm tougher because of your support.

To my publisher, Kensington/Dafina Books, and especially my editor, Mercedes Fernandez, what *dedication* you bestow on me. The time you've put into this series has meant a lot to me. I'm confident our efforts will bless many.

To my writing team, Jenell Clark, Christine Nixon, Dr. Deborah C. Thomas, Cassandra Brown, Dorcas Washington, Vanessa Davis Griggs, Victoria Christopher Murray, Sonya Jenkins, Edythe Woodruff, Beverly Jenkins, Joy Nixon, Chandra Dixon, Bridget Fielder, and Myra Brown Lee, what passion you teach me. Thanks for reading and giving me advice to help me piece all of my thoughts together. I'm blessed with zeal to get this message out because of the energy and excitement you have shown me about this project.

To my new family at Tyler Perry Studios, especially my producing team, Tammy Garnes and Ozzie Areu, what dreams you have helped me to obtain. Knowing that there is another medium out there for my books to touch even more souls fires me up. I'm flying amongst the stars because of the vision you helped me to realize with Georgia Sky.

To my babies, Dustyn Leon, Sydni Derek, and Sheldyn Ashli, what loyal followers you are. I thank you for always believing in me and for working so hard. I'm praying you keep giving God your all.

To my hubby, Derrick Moore, what love you show me. Thank you for allowing me the time to serve my sorority. I'm full of heart for others because you give me so much of yours.

To my readers, what a strong desire I have to inspire you. May the words in this book bless your soul. I'm wiser because I truly know we all need to strive to live each day to the fullest and I hope this read helps you do that.

And to my Almighty Father, what compassion you give to a sinner like me. May every person who turns these pages understand that as long as we please You, it doesn't matter whom we displease. I'm humbled by Your grace and I pray my work leads people to Your Son.

BETA GAMMA PI
TRADITIONS, CUSTOMS, & RITES

Founding Data

Beta Gamma Pi was founded in 1919 on the campus of Western Smith College by five extraordinary women of character and virtue.

Sorority Colors

Sunrise lavender and sunset turquoise are the official colors of Beta Gamma Pi. The colors symbolize the beginning and the end of the swiftly passing day and remind each member to make the most of every moment.

Sorority Pin

Designed in 1919, the pin is made of the Greek letters Beta, Gamma, and Pi. This sterling silver pin is to be worn over the heart on the outermost garment. There are five stones in the Gamma: a ruby representing courageous leadership, a pink tourmaline representing genuine sisterhood, an emerald representing a profound education, a purple amethyst representing deep spirituality, and a blue sapphire representing unending service.

Anytime the pin is worn, members should conduct themselves with dignity and honor.

The B Pin

The B Pin was designed in 1920 by the founders. This basic silver pin in the shape of the letter B symbolizes the beginning step in the membership process. The straight side signifies character. The two curves mean yielding to God and yielding to others. It is given at the Pi Induction Ceremony.

Sorority Flower

The lily is the sorority flower and it denotes the endurance and strength the member will need to be a part of Beta Gamma Pi for a lifetime.

Sorority Stone

The diamond is the sorority stone which embodies the precious and pure heart needed to be a productive member of Beta Gamma Pi.

Sorority Call

Bee-goh-p

Sorority Symbol

The eagle is the symbol of Beta Gamma Pi. It reflects the soaring greatness each member is destined to reach.

Sorority Motto

A sisterhood committed to making the world greater.

The Pi Symbol

The Bee insect is the symbol of the Pi pledges. This symbolizes the soaring tenacity one must possess to become a full member of Beta Gamma Pi.

Contents

BRIGHT

"So you think it's okay if somebody whacks you up-side the head, calls you all kinds of names, beats your behind, and who knows whatever else, Hayden Grant? I've even heard of cases where sororities make pledges perform some kind of sexual act," my mom Shirley voiced in anger, as my caramel face turned pale.

"Mom! I can't believe you would go there with me."

"What, Hayden? Don't be shocked. I know how bad you want to be a Beta and I know you might lose your mind to get what you want. Plus, you're about to be a sophomore in college, at a predominately African-American school. I know there are several nice-looking young men around grabbing your attention. Something made your grades slip last semester. I think you're still pure, but we need to talk about sex."

"I can't talk about this with my mom. I just can't," I said, shyly turning my head and twirling my mid-length do.

"Better she talk about it with you," my sister, younger by four years, popped into my room and said.

"Hailey, have you been standing there the whole time? Quit being nosy," my mom scolded and shooed her away.

"We were talking about being a Beta, Mom. We weren't talking about me and sex," I quickly reminded her.

"Well, I'm not done. I think any young lady that makes smart choices will do that across the board. If you make wise decisions, particularly when the alternative is giving it up to some boy who the next day probably won't know you exist. You could wind up pregnant or with some disease. Isn't it better to stay away from all that? Someone who's strong enough to resist temptation and stands for what God says is right, will not want to be a part of some group that thinks the only way you can get in is to participate in some form of illegal activity that the organization doesn't even tolerate," she said, getting louder and louder with each sentence.

"Okay Mom, I get it! You don't have to go on and on and on about it," I said to her, extremely frustrated.

I didn't want to go there with her, but it seemed to me like she needed to get her groove on. My dad Harry was away at war. He's an officer in the Navy and his girl had too much idle time on her hands. So much so that she was all up in my business.

My mom knew I wanted to be a member of Beta Gamma Pi ever since she pledged the organization's alumnae chapter when I was in the fifth grade. After she became a member, I remember many nights during my childhood when she was away with the service-oriented organization, working in the community by taking food to the poor, being there for the elderly, and helping the uneducated gain knowledge. Even though part of me resented not having all of her time, it just fueled me, excited me, and made me want to strive to become a member one day. My mom had wanted to pledge as an undergraduate when she was in college, but due to females tripping, she didn't. I had a deep longing to obtain that goal for her.

My mom came over and got right in my face. "Let me just tell you this really quickly. I desperately want you to be a Beta. But if you participate in any of that foolishness and anything happens, I don't want you calling me. I don't want you thinking that I can help save the line. None of that. Do you understand? I'm telling you now, I don't support hazing and in the end it only divides. Be a leader on that campus, Hayden Grant."

She went on to explain, for the fiftieth time, the legitimate steps to becoming a Beta. First, there was rush, where an informational session is held and the members of the organization explain all about what they stand for and what they do. They also distribute application packets to the prospective candidates, which need to be turned in by a certain date. After the packets are returned and reviewed by the members of the organization, then comes the interview. But not everyone will get one. After the interview, if you receive enough votes from the sisters of Beta Gamma Pi, then you become a part of the pledge line. After handing in the money for the pledge fee, a Pi induction ceremony is held. There are five gem ceremonies and an Eagle weekend hosted by the alumnae chapter, which pledges must attend. Next there is an intense week of studying the history of the sorority and a major exam is given before the candidates are ready to cross over and become sisters of Beta Gamma Pi.

"You participate in any other activity and it's hazing. Got it?"

I nodded. Of course I heard her, but I couldn't say what I would and wouldn't do once pressure from the Betas was applied. I didn't want to be ostracized and considered paper because I wouldn't participate in a few little uncomfortable things. I mean how bad could hazing really be, right?

There are certain rules that go along with the way many people think is the best way to pledge. First, pledging on the collegiate level carries more weight than pledging in an alumnae chapter. I thought this was crazy. However, the rationale is that collegiate chapters really make members do things *way* over and above what the standard rules call for. Also, many believe that if you don't go through the collegiate process then you are not a real pledge, only a *paper* one. And let's face it, if you have the chance, who wants to be called paper? Definitely not me.

Then there is the legacy rule. In some sororities if your mother is a member and you have the qualifications, then there is no vote necessary. You automatically become a member. But, with Beta Gamma Pi, that isn't the case. Since my mom didn't pledge on the collegiate level, their preferred methods, I knew I was going to have to pay for what she didn't go through. I was ready for it, because I knew if I made line I could legitimize my mom's place in the sorority.

"I'm gonna make you proud, Mom. You don't have to worry," I said, stroking her verbally and psychologically.

"Honey, all you need to do is concentrate on your grades and be the best Hayden you know how to be. If the Betas don't want you, it's their loss. You can always pledge the way I did," she said in a sweet tone, so I'd keep my hope. But I wasn't having it.

My mom wasn't all excited about the way she pledged. She knew the stigma attached to alumnae pledge methods. Though I knew deep in my heart that being put through an intense pledge process didn't make one a better member, if I had the opportunity to get all my props, I had to do it. Why would she think I wouldn't want all the respect?

My mother continued, "Now see, I can tell by your face you think pledging on the alumnae level is not kosher."

"Well, it was your dream to pledge undergrad," I quickly reminded her.

"Yeah, but just because that didn't work out doesn't mean that I would go back and trade my experience for anything. I was so connected with the ladies on my line. And quite honestly it was absolutely the best timing. God knew what He was doing. And Hayden, for you to have the outcome that He wants for your life, you have to ignore what others say and just focus on what is right. You know how to be a strong person, but a strong leader knows that God's way is golden. So seek Him and figure out what He wants for you. Plus, I truly now believe pledging on an alumnae level is the best way to join the organization," she said with her worried eyes locked on mine.

I smiled, feeling she believed those last words. I hugged her to let her know though I wanted a different experience, I was going to be okay. Then I was off to college. Western Smith University, here I come. It was time to get my sophomore year started.

We hugged, and then I was off. It was time to get my sophomore year started.

When I pulled up to the two-story apartment complex, I was ecstatic to see the cars of my three suitemates. Bridget was an over-the-top primadonna but she was cute with it though. Like me, she was from Little Rock, Arkansas. She had pretty banana colored skin and had a practically new, white Jaguar that went with her prim and proper personality perfectly. Clad in Sperry boat shoes, a lily pink Ralph Lauren polo shirt and a denim mini, Bridget was the fashion queen of our crew. We all admired her style. It seemed like she was up on the latest fashions even before they hit the stores. But for all her coolness, last year she had lunch with her mom three times a week. Who does that in college?

Then there was Myra. Our skin colors were in the same caramel brown family. She had a red Jeep shining in the lot. It wasn't brand new, but she took care of it. She was from Alabama, but her grandmother lived in Arkansas. Myra didn't sport the newest clothes, but I'd never seen hand-me-downs look so sassy. She was strong willed and loved having everything her way. Though that could be very annoying, I loved her.

And then there was the gorgeous dark mocha sister, Chandra. I guess out of all of them, she was my girl. She was so focused on her career goals—I longed to have her drive for a fulfilling life. Her black Ford Escort was on its last leg, but it was in the parking lot, which meant she was in the house. She turned heads all the time with her body-hugging ensembles. But I had to give it to her. The girl wore everything well.

Without even worrying about my bags, I grabbed my pocketbook and headed to the front door. Our apartment was the bomb. Each of us had our own spacious bedroom with freshly painted blond colored walls and full bathrooms to ourselves. We shared a joint kitchen and living room. None of us minded sharing these public spaces, but I think we all agreed that having our own private commodities was a nice alternative to living in last year's community dorms.

No more fresh meat on campus. We were sophomores. Yeah baby! We were really ready to change the world. We had our own place. We had big dreams. Now, we were ready to make them come true.

"Hey y'all!" I screamed when all three of them came to the door and gave me a hug.

Immediately, I could tell from their faces that something wasn't right. Something was definitely going on. *What now*, I thought. Myra and Bridget quickly headed into the living room.

"Dang, y'all got into it already?" I screamed out, madder than my dad would be if I'd told him I wrecked my brand new Cadillac CTS.

"It's the two of them," Chandra said, pointing away from herself. "Don't even look at me. I think they're crazy for even talking about them dumb sororities in the first place."

"Wait a minute, wait a minute, what's going on, girls?" I handed Chandra my purse and went over to Myra and Bridget. As I placed my arms around the two of them, I knew we couldn't have any beef this early. "Y'all, we've got our own place. We're not supposed to be arguing. We packed all that stuff away in the freshman year drama suitcase. I'm ready for a fresh start with my closest girls. I'm ready for us to have a super year. It's going to be a great time pledging Beta this year. There's no need to argue and fuss about when we're going to pledge now. They may not have a line this fall. But whenever they do, we'll be on it."

"You better tell her!" Myra said, looking at Bridget, removing my arm. "Because I now know Rho Tau Nu is the only way for me."

Okay, at that point I was really confused. Why was Myra talking about pledging the brown and peach? We hadn't had that in the plan. All last year we were at every single Beta Gamma Pi function. We didn't attend any other events. What was this?

"And that's where we are very different because I want to try and be a member of Mu Eta Mu, okay?" Bridget said to me. "I'm sick of that wench thinking her way is right."

"Who you calling a . . ." Myra uttered as she tried to reach over and strangle Bridget.

As I kept them apart, I scratched my head. Now my other girl was talking about wearing silver and gold? What in the world was going on? They knew the sunrise and sunset colors of lavender and turquoise were the colors we were going to sport.

So I turned around and looked at Chandra. "Help me out here! What are they talking about? What changed?"

"Um, again, I'm repeating—I don't know why y'all are thinking about any of them crazy sororities," Chandra said.

"Because they're founded on Christian principles," Bridget uttered, as she rolled her eyes at Chandra.

"And it's a great social organization to network and meet new people to do other big things, and it's a community service thing," I said. "But y'all . . . Beta Gamma Pi? I thought we were all going to be Betas? Everybody. All four of us."

"My mom's a Nu," Myra said.

"We know that, but you said you knew she'd been inactive all your life so they couldn't be about much," I said, reminding her of our conversation before we all went our separate ways last summer.

Myra just shrugged her shoulders. "Well, over the summer she joined a local chapter and I met a bunch of the ladies. They are professional women who really are making a difference in their careers. Plus, they are the largest sorority for a reason. Rho Tau Nu is doing major projects. RTN, Hayden. Sorry, girl. You can switch too."

Bridget grabbed my hand and said, "My mom's not Greek, but I've done a lot of research over the summer and Mu Eta Mu is for me."

"All of y'all are stupid," Chandra said.

"Just don't none of you talk to me," Myra said, going to her room.

"Like that will bother me," Bridget said as she went upstairs and slammed her door.

Chandra plopped on the couch and said, "All of you guys will need me before I need you. Those Greek letters will let you down. Trust me."

My world was caving in on me. Maybe we hadn't really finalized it, but in my mind it was already decided. Besides my three girls, I didn't care who else made the line. I had no other friends at Western Smith College. I'd only gone there because my Uncle Wade was the president of the school. I knew that a lot of people pledged sororities to get more status, to find themselves a clique. But I already had it going on in my own mind. My grades were good. My uncle didn't have to look out for me and I had the best group of girlfriends. But if we weren't going to pledge together the way I imagined it, if we weren't going to stand together—not only in a line but for causes to make the community better—did I want to do it alone?

And if there was any hazing, without my three girls, could I take it? I had walked into a mess and I had no idea how it could be straightened out.

Later that evening, I was at Wal-Mart buying my own groceries. No one in the house was talking to each other. Myra had put labels with her name on stuff in the refrigerator and Bridget had put all her items in one section. This was not how I thought our sophomore year was going to begin, but I needed to make sure I could eat, so I went out and got the necessary items.

As I came out of the store, a girl wearing a Beta Gamma Pi jacket turned to me and said, "Hey, we're having a party tonight. I'm sure you want to be there. Bring some friends!" she said, and handed me a flyer for the party.

I was caught off guard when she winked at me. Was the word out? Did every Beta know I wanted to be in their group? Or maybe all the events I attended last year did make a difference.

"You're planning to come, right? You know my name, don't you?"

Shoot, I knew she was a junior. I knew she was on the dance team. I knew I'd seen her before. This was all a part of pledging. It was an intimidation factor. The way she was staring at me like I'd better know her name was a lot to take in.

"Keisha! You're Keisha!" I said finally.

She looked me up and down. It was like she was bipolar. When she first approached me she was kind, now she was tripping.

"I'm Hayden," I said, as I extended my hand and she backed her arms away.

"I'll know your name when I need to know it. You coming tonight or what?"

I had a blank stare on my face. There was no way I could tell her that I wasn't coming. I didn't want to go to a party by myself, but I couldn't let her down either. She'd report back to the Betas and cross me off the list before I even got a chance to interview.

"I want to be there," I said nervously.

"Okay, I like you. You didn't know how to tell me no, but you told me something I wanted to hear. Smart. Alright. I'll look for you this evening. I know you won't let me down. If you do, you'll regret it, and that is a threat. Be scared," Keisha said, as she sharply turned and went to another group of girls clustered in the store handing out party flyers.

Coming back into the house, I yelled, "Hey everybody! Important apartment meeting."

"Apartment meeting? Where'd you get that from?" Chandra said, eyeing me down like I needed to check myself into the loony bin.

I looked at her and uttered, "I'm trying here, okay? Work with me, we don't need to have any discord or any strife. I figured out a way we can all push aside the tension."

"So Hayden, what you got to work this all out?" Chandra said, as Myra and Bridget walked into the living room.

"Let's go to a party!"

It took a minute, but then everyone started smiling. See, I knew my girls. We weren't the wild bunch, but we weren't duds either. We were sassy and cool.

"Whose party is it?" Chandra asked.

I didn't want to tell them that part because I didn't want to start another argument. So I took a breath, deeper than the ocean's bottom and hoped they would hear me out.

"Okay, you'll be doing me a favor. How about that?"

"The Betas are having a party?" Chandra said, completely disappointed. "I thought some guys were throwing this. I don't wanna party with a bunch of women."

"Well, if the girls are throwing it you know there are going to be tons of guys there," I said, lightly jabbing her in the arm.

"Alright, count me in," Myra said.

"Yeah, I'll go to a party. I'm sure the sisters of Rho Tau Nu are going to be there," Myra said. "I got to let them see how uninterested I am in anything the Betas are throwing."

"How will that happen if you're at the place?" Myra asked.

Myra smiled and responded, "I'll look bored."

"Yeah, I need to be there too because if any MEMs are in the house I need to let them see my face."

"Don't y'all think that's gonna be counterproductive?" Chandra said. "Aren't you only supposed to go to stuff that the organization you're interested in joining is throwing?"

"Ugh, it's not even like that, Chandra. You got sororities all wrong," I said, as the three of them stared me down. "Okay, well, I'm just saying we can change it. Just be ready in an hour, please?"

Sororities were territorial. It was rumored if you supported anyone else's events you were banned. Or at least you'd better have a good reason for giving other Greeks your time. I'd heard horror stories of one girl going to different rushes or informational sessions and in the end none of the sororites wanted her to pledge. Deep in my heart, I knew my crew were leaders. If we were in any group, we'd be open-minded and want our members to support worthwhile causes without feeling like someone would be dissing us if they did attend someone else's event.

As soon as we arrived at the student activity center on campus, which was about ten minutes from our apartment, we went off in different directions. I was a little upset. I wanted to hang out with my roommates and get them all to see that the way the Betas threw a party was a classic example of how awesome a group they were. I mean it just wasn't some back to school party. This was a bash. With decorations, food and slamming music—the Betas had set it out. The place was packed, the mood was right, and the lights were low. Girls were getting their groove on while all the guys were watching the swaying hips.

I looked across the room and saw a guy that caught my eye. It was Creed. I remembered him from the English and public speaking classes I took last year. I smiled, knowing that my sophomore year might bring a lot of challenges and things might not go exactly as I planned. But as I looked at the cutie heading my way, while being surrounded by Betas, I knew that my future for love and letters was bright.

2

GUIDANCE

"I knew I should have gotten your number before the summer break," said the divinely fine Creed.

My knees were starting to shake and I didn't want to smile too wide. He was gorgeous. Creed stood strong and masculine at five-foot-eleven. His white Crest smile offset his smooth, brown mocha skin. From his fresh line-up and fade to the seemingly perfect curl of his lashes, this man was eye candy! Even better, his presence was commanding, like that of royalty. The way he was looking at me from head to toe, I hoped that he was now single.

He beat me to the punch when he asked, "So what's up with you and Butch? Should I back away before he comes over and socks me?"

Butch was my ex-boyfriend from freshman year. Looking back, I must have been desperate to go out with him. He had an ego larger than three dorms put together. But besides that, he was a control freak and really into his fraternity, Pi Lambda Beta.

"Tell me something though, cause you know I'm trying to pledge Pi Lambda Beta and I don't want to speak to his girl. Getting kicked off line before I even make it would be something."

"I'm single. You know Butch and I were over last semester. It looks like it's going to be a crazy year for us both. I'm thinking about pledging too."

"For real? I know all of the sororities are going to try to snap you up," he said, as I noticed his eyes still checking me out.

Remembering he had a girl always glued to his hip last year and not wanting extra drama for myself, I said, "But you have a girlfriend too. Where's miss prim and proper?"

"I don't cheat. It's completely not my style. We're over, so since we're both free, that means we should give us a shot, right?"

I smiled. He stepped closer. Then he bent his head down toward my neck.

It was like Creed knew the DJ, because all of a sudden a slow song came on. He led me to the dance floor and we clung to each other's arms. His touch made me feel as if I were floating through the clouds.

"So you're really thinking about pledging, huh?" I said to him, trying to keep my mind off the fact that just being close to him and his fine body was turning me on in every way imaginable.

"You know you smell good, right?" he said to me, catching me off guard.

"You smelling my neck again?"

"You better watch it, soon I might be kissing it," he said, then licked his lips in a way that told me he wanted more.

Instinctively, I pulled back. I knew Creed pretty well, but how much I wanted him scared me.

"You pulling away. Do you want to stop dancing?"

"Yeah, it's getting a little hot in here."

As we walked off of the dance floor, I couldn't believe that he grabbed my hand. It wasn't a tight squeeze, and we weren't walking arm in arm, but he definitely had two of my fingers. And for a girl coming back to college with only books and pledging on her mind, this was a different ball game. Being with Creed put chills up and down my spine, and I knew that I really liked him. I had stepped into this place ready to impress the Betas and have fun with my roommates. Even though I was extremely bummed out that my suitemates went their own way, now I was happy my roommates could take care of themselves. And I certainly wasn't thinking about impressing anybody—except Creed. Creed had always impressed me, not only with his academic power, but his leadership skills were something awesome. He could give a speech that would motivate any crowd and he loved complimenting people. I had an appreciation for his skills and the way he'd bring out the best in people.

"I've always thought you were stunning. I can't believe you never noticed that I wasn't really studying during our study sessions last year. Instead, I found myself being caught up with how beautiful you were . . . and still are," he said.

"Okay, see, you were making me believe that you were

genuine and all of that stuff, but now you're giving me way too many compliments. I don't even deserve them. Stop," I said, hitting him on the knee.

"I ain't trying to freak you out, but I had a dream about you this summer, Hayden. Umm, let's just say, I'm a pretty happy guy to know that you and Butch are no more."

He was reaching over to kiss me, but before our lips could meet, Penelope Kent, the Vice President of the Betas, came over to me and said, "I need to talk to you now, excuse us."

She didn't give me a choice. She practically grabbed my arm. Then she yanked me away from Creed.

"I thought you wanted to pledge?" she said, once we were alone in the women's restroom. "Every function we had last year you were there. We even had the conversation about your mom's pledge experience. I went out on a limb for you and pegged you as my choice to make it. Did I waste my time thinking you'd be right for BGP?"

I didn't know what to do or say. I just knew it was put-up or shut-up time. I put all of my cards on the table. I said, "No, you didn't waste your time. I still want to be a Beta."

"Well, we don't want our girls all up in someone's face. We talked about this last year, girl. That's a no-no! Show some class and self-respect. Y'all looked like you needed to find a hotel or something, yuck! You've got a lot of work to do and we need to talk about this now. So meet me off campus at the Elks Club in fifteen minutes."

Before I could say anything, she left. I knew the clock was ticking. As it says in my mom's Beta handbook that I peeked at, the Vice President of the organization is the leader of the line. Penelope had spoken. Ticking her off wasn't going to help my cause. I had to figure out how I was going to respond.

Now it was on me. I had been given an order: either I could comply with it or ignore it. Make no mistake about it, whichever one I chose would pretty much determine my pledging fate.

I wasn't a rude person. I couldn't just walk out of the party without saying goodbye to Creed. We'd connected. How could I just leave him high and dry like that? And I certainly would have been pissed if he did it to me. However, if the Betas were watching me, I couldn't say goodbye or even explain to Creed what was going on. And in all honesty, I didn't know where things between Creed and me were headed. We were friends, even though he looked like he wanted to rip my clothes off and get busy. I certainly wanted more than that, but who could say a relationship was in store for us and could I afford to take that chance? I had wanted to be a member of Beta Gamma Pi for years and here was finally my opportunity. I had the grades. I had the community service. And I had the heart. Yeah, the Betas were acting crazy, I mean what was this secret meeting all about?

When I walked toward the exit, Chandra came up to me and said, "So okay, you just gonna bounce without saying a word? We came to this party because of you, girl. I can't believe you were about to leave! Come with me and bring the truth."

"Okay, okay," I said, motioning for her to come outside.

Chandra looked crazy and said, "If I go out they ain't gonna let me come back in."

"Yes, they will, just get your hand stamped by one of the Betas," I told her.

I took her hand and gave it to one of the Betas that I'd seen at the store earlier. Her large stature was so overwhelming and she looked even meaner than she did before. Her sweatshirt read, Soror Keisha, a mean machine. I couldn't imagine one person that she would vote to put on the line.

"What you looking at? I just want my hand stamped," Chandra said, just being real.

I could have hit my girlfriend in her side. Though she didn't want to pledge, I did. Now I was gonna get it for her smart comment. Keisha rolled her eyes at Chandra. And Chandra rolled her eyes right back at her. I was doomed.

When we got outside Chandra said, "What in the world is up with you taking their manipulation? See, I don't understand why you guys want to be a part of these sororities. These chicks think they own you guys or something. Well, they ain't gonna treat me like I'm stupid. I'm somebody with or without being a member of their group."

"It's to be expected. It's no big deal," I said, truly hoping I was right in what I was telling her.

"So, where you going? Why'd you bring me out here? What you got to say? Let me guess, one of them wants you to go to the store for more punch or something?" Chandra teased.

Trying not to get upset I said, "I can't tell you, but I do have to go and meet a couple of them."

"That's crazy. You about to walk on this campus by yourself. Girl, don't we have security? That's just asking for trouble—you're wearing a short dress practically up your behind and then you're going to prance around campus at midnight?"

"I know this sounds crazy, but this is something I really want to do. Please tell . . ."

She cut me off and said, "Look, I ain't seen Bridget and Myra. I don't know where they are. I'm about to roll out myself in a minute. But we came over here with you, if you leave now how we gonna get home?"

"Shoot, I've got to be there in three minutes," I said, noticing how much time had passed since Penelope summoned me. "Look, just make sure they get home. Please tell them what happened. I know they'll understand."

She grabbed my wrist. "I'm staying up and I'll call the cops if you aren't home in a few hours. Where are you meeting them?"

I gave her all of the particulars and hugged her tight. One thing I liked about Chandra was that she knew who she was. I'm not saying that I wanted to be a Beta because I needed an identity, but I loved the fact that she felt she was fine just the way she was. No clubs, no sororities—none of that stuff. I was almost there. There was just one more thing left that I needed to make myself complete . . . Greek life.

"So look, could you also tell Creed that I said goodbye? You remember him, he was my study partner last year."

"Yeah, I saw you talking to him. I'll handle it. Go girl, and be careful."

I got to the Elks Club a couple of minutes late. Surely, that couldn't be a big deal. I was really scared, yet I knew I wanted to do this. I was strong and I wasn't going into the room alone. I'd take my Savior with me, and with Him by my side I knew I could do this.

When I walked into the abandoned Elks Club, a spotlight shined on me. The room was freezing. I felt like my stomach was falling to the floor. What had I gotten myself into? This was eerier than a horror flick.

One girl shouted, "You're two minutes late, drop down and give me fifty push-ups."

I smirked, certain they were joking, right? Suddenly, ten girls surrounded me with Beta Gamma Pi gear on. I looked around and saw that big Keisha, the girl from the party, was looking right at me.

As if I couldn't hear, she shouted, "You hope that I am your big sister one day. But I'm not now. So, don't look at any of us. You hold your head down. Stand on one leg and think about why you want to be a Beta."

Another girl said, "Penelope told us you were all over some guy at our party. If you want to be a member of our organization, we only take the best. We don't accept girls with fast reputations."

Then another voice chimed in and said, "You don't need to wear all of that makeup either. It's natural beauty we're interested in."

"GPA better not drop," a girl yelled, as she jammed me in the side. "We already know it's a 3.69. You can make it a 3.75."

I was so shocked. How did they have this kind of information on me? I hadn't turned in an application packet. Maybe this hazing thing was going to be more than I ever imagined it would be. All this preliminary stuff, being underground as the Greeks called it, was supposed to be minimal, but they were practically stalkers.

Someone else pushed me and said, "Make sure you are at all of our events, no chit-chatting in the hallways, just go to and from class, and take yourself home. And make sure not to wear any more clothes that make it look like you're not wearing any. Can you do that?"

Another echoed, "Can you do that? Do you want to be a Beta?"

My leg was starting to buckle and the room was starting to spin, but I knew I had to give them an answer, so I shouted as loud as I could, "YES, I CAN DO IT. I WANT TO BE A BETA!"

"That's all we wanted to hear. Cool," Keisha said, before they all left me standing there in the cold, dark room alone.

I fell to the ground, really wondering if I had what it takes to make it.

It had been two weeks since that crazy meeting in the Elks Club that left me feeling full of intimidation and fear. I hadn't seen another Beta since that time, but I made sure I went home and followed the instructions they gave me that night.

I'd go straight to class, not even stopping for a bite to eat on campus. I didn't have time to waste. After class, I was in my room studying. It wasn't like I didn't care about what was going on with my roommates, but I knew if they needed me they would let me know.

Creed was in my packed psychology class. I tried as much as I could not to let my eyes roam to his seat. I managed to get out of class quickly so he couldn't stop me and say anything. But on this particular day I couldn't find my keys. And I wasn't one to get to my car and start looking for my keys—no, I was the type who needed to have everything ready.

As I dug in my purse, his sexy voice said, "Okay, so are you avoiding me or what?"

"Avoiding you?" I looked up at him and replied.

"Oh, come on now, Hayden, since your girl told me you had to jet out of the party I haven't even been able to find you. I don't even have a phone number to call. I saw you in class twice last week, but before I could even say anything you were gone. I made sure I caught you this time. I just wanted to know, why can't we talk? Let me know and I'll back away." He took his hand and touched my cheek. "It may kill me that I can't make you my girl, but I'll respect your decision. Just be woman enough to tell me to my face that it was over before it even began, you know?"

I didn't know how to react. Should I take the gamble? I hadn't stopped thinking about him and now that I had an inkling that he just didn't want a fling, maybe I needed to invest in him too.

"I know this is going to sound completely crazy, but I'm hungry," I said finally, giving us a try.

Smiling, Creed said, "Yeah, let's go to the café and get something to eat."

"Uh, no! Can you meet me at the Cracker Barrel off the interstate?"

"Way out there? Are you serious?" he groaned.

"Would I make such a crazy suggestion if I wasn't serious?"

"Fine, but can we ride together?"

I shook my head. I wanted a bite to eat. I didn't want to be obligated. What if our time alone didn't feel right? And what if the Betas were watching? Nope, I needed to drive myself.

"Alright, well I don't have any more classes, do you?"

"Nope, this is my last one too. I can meet you there in twenty minutes."

"Alright, let me give you my number, just in case."

I opened my notebook and wrote down my cell phone number. Instead of just handing him the paper, I had to be discreet, so I looked around and was relieved that no one was watching. As I walked by him I said, "That's for you." And I left the piece of paper with my number on top of my desk and walked out of the classroom.

Driving over there I didn't know how to feel. On the one hand, Creed was fine. But on the other, dating him wasn't my goal, becoming a Beta was. However, if a golden ticket falls into your lap, you can't throw it away without opening it. I was giddy and open-minded. Ready for whatever Creed and I may turn out to be.

When I entered the restaurant, Creed, who was seated at a booth, quickly got up, walked over to me and said, "Good to see you," and then kissed me on the cheek.

As we walked toward the booth, I was surprised to see a lily at my place setting.

"This is for me?"

"Yeah, don't you need it for what's going on now?"

"What do you mean?" I asked.

"The Betas are working you. I'm just giving you their sorority flower. Just so you know, just like a lily can sustain much, so can you."

"Aww, you just don't know how good it feels that you know." I reached over and gave him a big hug. "This is so much, I mean I'm not even on line and I have to watch everything that I do."

"They don't want you talking to guys, huh?"

"No, they don't, and I'm so paranoid. I don't know if they have spies watching me or what, and I didn't want to make time for you if we want two different things."

"What, you just thought I wanted to hit it and run?"

"Well, let's just be open and honest about these things with each other, why don't we?" I said sarcastically. "But on the real, I'm not trying to rush into anything."

He stroked my hand and said, "Cool, tell me what's on your mind. That is the only way we can have anything, by being honest with each other. So what's up? You want to pledge, right?"

"Yeah."

"Well, if pledging is something you want to do, then we can work around that. I like you a lot and I have liked you since last year. I know who you are, what you stand for, and I want to be with you however I can."

Trying to keep it together I said, "Did you ever think pledging would be so crazy that we would undergo this underground foolishness?"

Before he could answer, my ex-boyfriend, Butch, walked up to the table. I could see on Creed's face that he was intimidated and extremely uneasy. Though Creed had more muscle, Butch held the letters.

"What's up, lady?" He reached down and tried to kiss me.

I immediately jerked away. First, we were not together anymore, and second, his breath stank.

"Oh, so it's like that?" Butch said.

"It's been like that for a long time, Butch. We're eating, do you mind?"

"Uh, dude, you might want to think about it. You can't be my fraternity brother and take my lady. You might want to be a smart man, leave her alone and take heed to my guidance."

PLEDGING

I could see the sweat falling from Creed's brow as Butch laughingly walked away. I knew he was pissed about being called out, but he knew he couldn't have gone off on Butch.

"Here, you need this napkin?" I said to him. I could see he was stressing.

"Naw, naw, I'm straight," he replied, trying to act as if Butch hadn't bothered him at all.

It was interesting because he'd been so nice until Butch showed up. Now, when he was faced with choosing his goal to pledge a fraternity over me, it wasn't as easy as he thought.

"Listen, just like I told you, seriously Butch and I are through. Way through. He's a jerk, and he crossed a couple of lines. It's over. You don't have to worry about any of that."

"Really, I'm straight," he responded.

"I can see you're not straight. You're fidgeting. You're acting weird. I've been around you for a long time and I've never seen you come apart at the seams like this."

"Wait, I'm together. What you trying to say?" Creed asked like he was offended.

"No need to be defensive. I'm just calling a spade a spade. You said throw the cards out on the table and be truthful, right?"

"Yeah."

"Well, calm down. Let's talk about this. I know what you want. I'm feeling the same pressure. Pledging is hard, and if we gotta put whatever we have going on on the back burner, then I'm down to do that. You're not gonna hurt my feelings."

"If y'all are through, Hayden, then forget him," Creed said, looking to see if Butch had driven off.

"I hear you talkin', but your actions are singing a different tune."

He got up from his seat and came over to my side of the booth. Instinctively, I slid over. He put his arm around me and turned my jaw to his, looked me in my eyes and winked.

Creed said, "It's something about you. I gotta pursue this. Yeah, I've wanted to be a Pi for so long, but if I let you go I will probably regret it for the rest of my life. Why do I have to make a choice because some jerk, who's mad that he let you go, tells me I have to? Yeah, he has something I want but I know I got something he wants too. I'd be an asset to his fraternity. All of the fraternities want me. I'm just keeping it real. Butch is a jerk, but he ain't stupid. You gotta know your own worth too."

"How do you know people want you like that?" I asked, very intrigued to know if fraternities handled things differently.

"They been coming at me trying to sell me on why they're the best. What they stand for, like I haven't done my homework. I don't know. I want to be a Pi and I want to wear brown and green."

"Well, at least you know a lot of people want you. I'm starting to doubt now if even the Betas want me," I told him as a waitress came with our sandwiches.

"Naw, that can't be true. I hear girls talking all the time. I'm in different circles, and if they haven't stepped to you yet, you just wait. They all gonna make their claim. This is rush time. They're going after the hottest sophomores and juniors who aren't in a fraternity or sorority. Everybody's gonna be staking their claim. You just gotta know how to play your cards when they step to you."

"What do you mean?"

"Well, I mean you don't want to show your hand too early. You got to keep everybody guessing."

"I went to see the Betas the other night."

"Oh, so that's where you went."

"No, I didn't mean I really went to see them."

"No need to cover it up. You sorta gave it away earlier. You're just confirming it. When other sororities come to you, if you know you want to pledge Beta, then you got to respectfully decline. Not tick them off or make them upset. If you do, they'll blackball you and even the Betas won't want you. You got to make everyone think you respect their sorority, but not be so interested. Make them intrigued to find out who you are. Just don't go over the top to please them."

"And if a Beta catches me in one of those conversations?"

"You just got to pretend that they're watching at all times. Be politically correct. Sometimes these Greeks work together to solidify candidates. They go way back, and work together to help the community."

"What do you mean?"

"If they know you have been to their event, they're gonna have somebody else come to you trying to see if you're really solid," Creed said, very knowledgeable about the whole Greek game.

"If we want to pledge 'cause we want to do good for the community, be in a Christian organization, have a common bond with folks, try to be the best we can be with a bunch of smart folks, then why does there have to be all these crazy standards that are not even at all a part of the equation? You and I are in psychology class together and even the best case studies don't have folks going through stuff like this to find out if they are loyal."

He chuckled. "I know you didn't think pledging was gonna be easy, did you?"

"No, I didn't."

"Well, get ready for the ride. I think it's going to be worth it though. You can't change the game from the start, but once we're in it, we can make all the rules."

Impressed by his knowledge and philosophy of Greek life, I said, "So, then, are we going to try this dating thing? You're not goin' to get intimidated?"

"We might have to sneak around so I don't offend your ex, but I'm calling the shots. If you're in it, I'm in it."

He didn't take his eyes off me as he leaned in and kissed me. It felt good that we agreed to try.

Leaving psychology class the next week, I was having the toughest time catching up to Creed. We said we would play it low so that no one would know we had something going on. We had our discreet ways of walking a couple steps behind one another or walking side by side. We would text each other—at least when we had distance between us—but this day the brother was gone. Of course that baffled me. Where was he off to so fast that he couldn't even say hello? And why was he sitting in class all day wearing ridiculous shades when it was dreary out? When we got outside of the building, I didn't even care if anyone was watching me. I sprang toward him and touched his shoulders.

When he turned around I said, "Okay, so why are you dodging me and why are you in class wearing shades?"

As he quickly began to turn away, I grabbed the glasses. I needed his attention.

"Don't do that!" he screamed out.

It was actually scaring me that he was being so defiant. Even worse, though, I was horrified when I saw the bruise around his eye.

"Okay, so what's goin' on? What's up with that?"

"I gotta go. I can't talk to you right now. Please just give me the glasses."

I stepped back. There should be no marks on anyone's

body because of some pledge bull. I wasn't having it and if I had to tell my Uncle Wade to get justice, I would.

I demanded, "No, you're not getting them until you tell me what's going on."

"Hayden, I appreciate your concern, but I'm not a lil' baby, okay. You can keep the shades, do what you gotta do, but I gotta go."

"No!" I said grabbing his arm. "Wait, please, I care about you. You know I do, talk to me. Who did this?"

He saw in my eyes that I knew he received the bruise from pledging. What were we signing up for?

"Don't look like you don't understand why I'm enduring all of this. Butch told me he's got guys everywhere."

To heck with Butch. I went over and put my hand on his cheek, trying desperately to reach his eye. Creed jerked his head back.

"I'm a tough boy. I got this, for real."

"Creed, I'm not saying you don't, but that's not what this is supposed to be about. We're not trying to join an organization whose main purpose is brutality. I'm gonna tell the school's president. This isn't some gang initiation here. You've got something to offer. I want to be a Beta more than I want all A's this semester, but I will not let them hit . . ."

Before I could finish my statement, he said, "Hayden, you'll tell nobody. Plus, you are talking a lil' too fast, a lil' too early, a lil' too soon. You don't know what you'll do until you are in that room. All that pressure coming at you from all different sides will have you crazy. Your head is gonna be spinning and your line sisters are gonna be depending on you to stay strong. If you're not in it, if you're not ready, if you don't think you can take a lil' something, then you better get out from the fire cause they certainly turn the heat up."

I just shook my head, unable to digest what he was really telling me. His bruise looked so bad. He needed a steak on it, ice, something. No way could Creed think this was okay at all. But I was going to respect his wishes, I wasn't going to tell anyone what happened to him.

"I'll text you later, okay?" he said, leaning in and giving me a kiss.

I didn't want him to go. That exchange between us was true bonding. I could feel the vulnerability, and the rawness in his heart. He was going through something awful trying to become a member of Pi Lambda Beta.

"What the heck am I thinking?" he said, quickly pulling away. "Girl, you gonna make my other eye get tore up," he said as he looked over his shoulder.

"Did Butch do that?" I said, finally touching the tender black-and-blue bruise.

"Ouch," he said.

I gently rubbed his bruise. I wanted us to be far away from any distractions. I was just a girl, liking a boy, wishing we could have time without drama.

"Umm, that feels good, but I gotta go, Hayden. I'll text you. I'm okay. That kiss you gave me is gonna make me endure any little thing Butch wants to throw my way. But, I will tell you this."

"What?"

"He threw your relationship with him in my face and

said he had you in every way, and, uh, it sorta made me push him, so he punched me. For some reason, all our talks last year, I just assumed . . .”

“That I was a virgin?” I interrupted, hoping he really knew me. “I am, and at this point with all this stupid pledging stuff you and Butch are doing, neither one of you is going to change that.”

I was angry hearing they were talking about me in some dumb hazing session. Though Creed thought it was honorable, I wanted to be left out of it. I tossed his shades to him and stormed off.

I didn’t know who I was really mad at. But how could Butch lie like that and why did Creed think he needed to defend my honor? What, did he think it was true? I hadn’t even started pledging and it hurt already. It seemed like maybe the whole pledging idea was a dumb one.

“So, the Betas are having a self-esteem forum and you’re not going?” Chandra said to me as she came into my room with Bridget and Myra.

I missed the friendship the four of us used to have, but now in our sophomore year, not even a full semester into it, we were so far apart. We never spent time together. We never talked about anything. To see the three of them come into my room because they thought something was wrong with me, as I lay across my bed, feeling completely perplexed, touched me.

“I can’t believe she’s not going,” Myra said.

“Girl, you know they gonna be looking for you because they know you want to pledge and put them Beta Gamma Pi letters on your jacket this spring. You know they want you to show up for some of their stuff, but if they want you, you're not automatically blackballed because you're not there. You could be studying for a major test or something. Relax if you want, girl," Chandra said. "That's why I'm not pledging nothing. A lot of the fraternities around here already got underground lines going. Boys falling asleep in class. They can't wear nothing but a white long sleeve shirt and khaki pants. You can tell the ones. I'm not letting no female strip away my dignity."

"That's just it though, y'all," I said, finally sitting up as I stared up at my ceiling.

"It's not supposed to be about any of that. I've been researching the history and all these organizations were founded back in the early nineteen hundreds. That's when black folks didn't have many rights and they formed these organizations to come together, to make a difference in the community, to stand on God's word, to get a good education and uplift one another. All this bashing, all this, 'You better do what I say or hit the highway' mentality, just defeats the whole purpose."

"What are you talking about, Hayden? You sound like you want to go pick up a picket sign and go march or something," Myra said.

"Naw, she got a point," Chandra said, truly feeling what I meant. Greek organizations needed to be about their founders' business and not foolish business.

"We don't understand what it was like to live back then, and if we just let our minds focus on the injustice, the racism, inequality, and the segregation that still exist in a lot of America, they wouldn't be tripping about recruiting members for public service organizations that are suppose to change that."

"Yeah, that's true," Bridget said, as she got up and left the room.

"Where is she going?" Myra said.

"I'm sure she is going to fix some tea or something," Chandra said, as the three of us laughed.

Bridget was a young, black, hip Martha Stewart. She believed in girl-talk over tea and cookies. Though we laughed, we all wanted her pampering.

"I just don't know how much I will be willing to endure. If I know how crazy it is on this end and I'm still thinking about doing it, what does that say about my character? What does that say about me?" I said, scratching my head.

Myra leaned down beside me and replied, "You know you can get in there and change it all. Every organization isn't perfect. If they were, why would they need any new members? I have been looking up RTN's history too. They have a program that is out of this world to me. They focus on so many positive things, it made me realize the sisters are really together. Now I'm convinced I want to be a part of them."

"And if your head gets bashed in the process, you still want to rock their colors?" Chandra said.

"I just think a lot of that pledging hype people throw out there is overrated. I want to get on the line and see. That's where the sisterhood and bond comes in with your line sisters. You gotta go through something to get tight, right?" Myra said.

Chandra and I said "Wrong!" at the same time.

"How can you love somebody that's giving you hell? How can you forget what they did to you, how they demeaned you and belittled you and then you call them sister?" Chandra said.

Bridget came to the door with a tray and four mugs of steamy, cozy chamomile tea. She even had sugar cookies as well. Myra and I quickly reached for ours.

"We love you, girl," Myra said to Bridget.

"I just felt like this was a tea moment. The four of us have been so busy doing so much, that we haven't been making time for each other. I hope I make the Mu Eta Mu line, but I can't imagine loving my sisters more than I love the three of you guys," she said, as we all took a tea cup and clicked them together. "Nothing will tear us apart."

"Well, Myra, I know you're going to be a Nu, Bridget, you're goin' to be an MEM, and Hayden, you're going to make the Betas stronger no matter what the cost," Chandra added.

"Who says we're going to make it?" Bridget said, looking away.

Chandra smiled and raised her mug. " 'Cause I know you guys, and God answers prayers. You're strong and you'll do this for Him. That sorority stuff isn't for everybody, but that doesn't mean I don't support what you're doing or why you want to do it. Y'all are awesome. So here's to pledging."

BRUTAL

Having an uncle who is the president of the college you attend may seem like a big deal but for me it wasn't. Thankfully, he stayed out of my way and I stayed out of his. Well, that was until he summoned me to his office during class. Most people didn't know we were related because we had different last names, but now they surely knew something was up when he sent a messenger to get me. I didn't really like that. I just wanted to be normal. If I only saw him on holidays or when I needed money was fine with me.

"Hey Hayden," his secretary said. "He's in a meeting right now."

"No, he just called for me to come here. I'm gonna see him," I said, opening up the door to his office.

I was stunned when I opened the door and saw my aunt's hands around my uncle's throat. I didn't know what was going on, but his secretary was right. I wasn't supposed to see this.

Unsure how to react, I said, "Sorry to interrupt, but Uncle Wade, you called me."

The two of them went to separate sides of his office. I'd never seen my uncle look so distraught. Obviously, the tension lingering in the air was a sign that this whole incident was serious. His wife, stuck-up Aunt Anne, as my sister and I always called her, grabbed her purse as she grunted. She fled past me, brushing my arm.

"Hayden, now you know you gotta knock," my uncle said, trying to play it off.

"Okay, what was that all about?" I went over to him and demanded. He ignored me, got on his phone and blasted his secretary.

"I told her you were busy, sir," I heard her say.

"Are you and Aunt Anne having problems? Was she beating you?" I asked when he hung up the phone. I couldn't believe I was asking the toughest man I knew such personal questions, but I'd seen for myself what was going on, and it didn't look right.

When he didn't respond, silence came over the room. All my life he'd played the protective role in my life. My mom's younger brother had schooled my high school boyfriends when my dad was overseas traveling. Now, I felt like I needed to protect him.

"I didn't think I was interrupting, because you got me from class," I said, still unable to shake the images I'd seen moments before.

"Okay baby, you're a sophomore in college now, a big girl. You know adults have issues," he said, still unable to look at me.

"Oh really? I've forgotten how married couples interact. My dad's been away for so long now," I said, getting a little sad.

"I know," he said, coming over to give me a hug.

I truly missed my father, but he was an officer in the United States Navy. When it was time for him to go, he had to go. When it was time for him to come home, he often stayed overseas. It was more than duty to him. It was his life. He'd write, call and say he loved me, my mom and Hailey. However, how could that be the case when he was often away? I had a small family, my sister was four years younger than me and my mom had her own life. I was happy to be away at college trying to find my way and later tonight I would finally have that opportunity. There were flyers all over campus, tonight was rush night. I had waited for so long. Pledging would extend my family and I was excited about that.

"Look, don't you go telling your mom about what you saw here between your aunt and me, okay? Everything's fine. She and I just—well, everything's fine."

"Naw, it's cool. I won't say a word. Whatever you say," I told him. "Why'd you want to see me though?"

"Your mom told me that you were about to pledge. I know all the sororities are having their rush tonight and I'm just trying to make sure this is seriously something you want. A lot of girls think it is and end up getting in way over their heads. These sororities and fraternities nowadays can get off track if they have the wrong members leading. So many of them are in so much trouble. We just want to make sure you know what you're doing,"

"I was just standing here thinking that if I can become a member of Beta Gamma Pi, that would be a dream realized for me. This is the beginning. Going to rush is not me signing up to be a member of anything. I'm not sure I'm going to do it," I said, giving him the answer I knew he wanted. "You've got a smart niece. Let me go and evaluate it. I won't let you down."

"I'd like to be able to look at you and say that everybody does their pledge process by the book. However, that wouldn't be true. Even on my campus, I'm not oblivious to the fact that craziness goes on. I try to crack down on it. I meet with the advisors, my faculty and staff, and I even talk to the presidents of each of the chapters. But if people want to have stuff messed up, they will. If they know they can get away with doing stupid things, they'll do that too."

Being real with him, I asked, "I'm just curious why my aunt thinks it's okay to put her hands around your neck. Has that happened before? Does she think she can get away with it?"

"Come on, Hayden. Drop it, okay? Your uncle can take care of himself. I run this big ol' school, right?" He kissed me on the forehead, opened the office door and shoved me out.

I sighed. I hoped he really could take care of himself. My family had issues.

The Betas had their rush, an informational session to tell potential pledges all about their organization. The meaningful event was held at an exquisite restaurant not far from campus. Lavender and turquoise candles were lit everywhere. On one side of the room sat the sisters of Beta Gamma Pi and on the other side were all of the hopefuls, like me. They had a small stage set up with a mic and everything. But I just kept wishing that someone I knew would walk through the door.

Before I left our apartment, as hard as I tried to convince Chandra to come with me, she held true to the fact that she was not going to pledge. Myra got dressed wearing anything but brown or peach because she went to the Nu rush. And Bridget wanted to show the MEMs she looked great in silver and gold. Despite what we tried to tell her, she went out of the door sporting their colors to their rush.

As I stood alone, I had to stand tall in my mind. I watched the different ladies of the sorority look me up and down. No one was smiling until I saw Penelope, who was the Vice President of the chapter and head of the line.

She came over to me and said, "You're going to be fine."

"I don't know. I don't think your sorority sisters like me very much," I said as I grew even more uncomfortable with the way Keisha was eyeballing me.

"Oh they like you a lot, trust me. Some of these other girls in here may have to worry. But of course they have to be tough on you. The Chapter President's about to come up and introduce herself, so sit!"

"Hi, I'm Edythe Stone, the Chapter President," the confident girl with short sassy hair said to the audience of approximately forty. "Welcome to the Beta Gamma Pi rush. It's obvious that you all are curious about our wonderful sorority. Today we're just here to make sure that you leave without any doubts that Beta Gamma Pi is definitely something you want to be a part of. Founded in 1919, here, on the campus of Western Smith, five women were impressed by the sororities being established in the east for equality and change. With lots of injustices in the central part of the country as well, they came together and decided to take a stand. Pi Lambda Beta was also founded that same year here. Make no mistake about it though, the men decided to get behind their women and join them in the cause, but of course they couldn't be in the sorority so they formed a fraternity to help."

A very short girl I noticed was taking notes. I didn't know if I should be doing the same. Certainly, I didn't want to miss or forget anything.

Edythe continued, "Beta Gamma Pi stands on five key points and everything we do is around those five things: leadership, sisterhood, education, spirituality and service. We build up leaders. We believe the bond of sisterhood is the essence of our survival and education is how we build our strength. We're a Christian-based organization that believes in serving the public from our heart. I believe most of you already got it going on, but if you want to join a dynamic group of women ready, empowered, charged, motivated and determined to make a difference in this world that we live in, then this sorority is for you. If you seek to be a part of a group of women who want to make this world better than they found it, then this sorority is for you. If your heart is big and you're not the center of your own world, then maybe . . . just maybe, you too can be a Beta."

"Like they don't need us," I heard a girl behind me say.

I almost wanted to turn around and tell her to be quiet. She was going to ruin her chance. Though I knew it was highly unlikely, I was down with us all making it.

"Trisha, hush!" I heard a chick next to her say.

"What, Chris? You know I'm telling the truth."

Penelope held up a white 8 x 10 envelope and said, "If you are interested, please pick up an application packet before you leave. You must have a letter of recommendation by a member of our sorority, two letters showing you've consistently done community service, and didn't just start last week. Also, the twelve-page application itself must be typed and we need your official transcript. All of this needs to be in one week from today to the place specified on the packet."

She also went on to tell us each packet would be scored and if we got enough points we'd get an interview. If we got enough points after that then we'd be invited to be on their line. I had a feeling this was going to take much more work than I could have imagined. Looking at the Betas I knew they weren't impressed easily.

Then the chapter advisor got up and started talking about the academic requirements involved in us getting into the organization. That Trisha girl behind me just kept talking though.

"Whatever. I know I have a 2.5 GPA, but it's not like they don't want me to be on their line. Are you kidding?"

Someone from the other side of the room said, "Hush!" loudly, a little too loudly. Then five of the Betas got up from their seats and came to our side, giving us intimidating glares.

When we were dismissed and had time to mingle, I couldn't believe three of the Betas cornered me and asked me why was I talking during their presentation. Thankfully, Penelope came over and escorted me away from the heat.

"It wasn't me!" I said to her, feeling like they hated me.

"They know it wasn't you. You were in the front row. We could all see you weren't talking. Plus, you were sitting all by yourself. You gotta know how to handle them. But we all have a favorite in the room and I really like you," Penelope said.

"Why?" I asked her.

"Because of all the girls I've talked to that say they want to be Betas, you outshine them all. Their reasons for wanting to pledge are shallow. They say to wear the letters, to sport the colors, to try to get guys, I mean you wouldn't believe some of the stupid stuff they say. And even though I know you are a legacy . . . Yeah, we know," she said, seeing the tension on my face.

I wished I could have kept that a secret. I'd always heard mixed things about being the daughter of a Beta. Either that gave you an edge, or the chapter members would cast you out because they felt you were too cocky. I didn't know what would be my fate if they found out so I kept it low key.

"Your roommates are all trying to pledge something different, and yet you still want this. I saw you pushing a guy in a wheelchair the other day down the hall to class. Somebody else dropped their books and you were there to help them out. I don't know. You have outstanding character. The character we need in our group. I'm happy you came to rush tonight. I'm glad the night after our party didn't deter you." I reached over to hug her and she backed away. "I'm not that glad. I'm not just gonna hand you my letters. You're going to have to work for them. You ready to work for them, Hayden?"

I nodded.

"Cool."

I hoped it was.

The next evening, I was home working on a paper for my psychology professor, Dr. Griffin. The dude was so rigid, he needed a female to loosen him up. It felt like school had just started and I was already weighed down with work. Then my doorbell rang, giving me the break I needed. "Come on, we gotta go!" a familiar voice said to me as I opened my apartment door and got yanked out of it.

"Wait a minute. I don't have my purse, my wallet or my keys. What's this about?"

"Okay, I'm Trisha. I'm trying to pledge Beta. We've been instructed to come and pick you up. You in this or what?"

Now, I understood. I guess the crazy rollercoaster ride of pledging was on. I held up my finger to say one minute. Part of me was excited. At least this time I wouldn't be around the crazy girls alone.

"I'll be at the car," Trisha said.

"Sounds good. I'll be right out."

When I went inside to get my purse Chandra yelled out, "Hayden, who's that at the door?"

"It's nobody," I said quickly, truly not needing her to act like a parent.

"I know you not going underground," she said as I looked away. "All right, hard head. Don't get your head smashed in."

"I'll be back later. Don't worry," I said to her.

"Take your phone!"

"Alright, alright, I'm straight," I said, as I opened the front door.

"I'm writing down the license plate of this girl's car. You don't even know her!"

I blew a kiss and she smiled.

I went out to Trisha's car and got in the back. It was tight. But I wasn't going to complain.

Trisha's trying to pledge too. I mean how much trouble could I get in, really?

When I got in the car with the other three girls, no one said hello. Maybe we all had knots in our stomachs.

"I can't believe you had to pick me up. It's tight back here. I could have driven," the plus-size girl sitting with me in the backseat complained as I strapped in.

Trisha was driving and replied, "You can get out of my car and walk for all I care. But I'm the one with the instructions and directions. They said follow them completely and that's what I'm doing."

The two of them argued back and forth. It was madness. One thing I learned from psychology class is how to analyze people. It looked like both Trisha and this other girl were strong people. Sitting beside Trisha in the front passenger side of the car was a girl who introduced herself as Kellie.

I responded by introducing myself as well, and then said, "Hey guys, don't we all want the same thing? If we're about to walk into the lion's den with the Betas, shouldn't we all be on the same side?"

"And she speaks," Trisha said.

"Yeah, how can you be at the rush and not try to meet anybody? I'm Bea, by the way," the larger girl said to me.

"That was the advice I got," I said to them. "Listen and stay low-key."

"Well, the President, Edythe, likes me and she told me that I should have allies," Bea said.

Thinking about this I took a deep breath and said, "So, now we know that it's not just what they tell one of us that matters. We now have to compile what they say to a few of us and decipher what it all really means."

"Oh yeah, I see," Bea said, "they'll tell each of us something different and we gotta put it together to make sense of it. They're forcing us to work together."

I nodded. This was going to be more work than I ever thought. Mind games were something.

We pulled into the parking lot that Trisha had been instructed to go to. Four other cars were there waiting. It looked like people were in those cars. None of us in Trisha's car wanted to exit.

"So what, are we just supposed to sit here?" Bea said.

No one had answers, so we sat. All of a sudden, my cell phone rang. I looked at it and saw it was Penelope. I answered.

"Yes, I understand," I said to her as she confirmed that we were in a parking lot with four other automobiles.

She gave me twenty minutes to get everyone to a new location. But we had to be in uniform. Once I explained that to the girls in my car, we panicked, thinking there was no way that could happen.

"They want us to go twenty miles from here, and be there in twenty minutes, dressed alike?" Bea said.

"We've got to figure out a way to do this," Trisha said.

I stepped out of the car and motioned for everyone to get out of the other cars too. After I explained our task, everyone was talking at once. There was no way we could devise a plan. We lost two minutes just trying to figure the whole thing out.

So I yelled out, "How many people got a few dollars on them? We gotta pass Wal-Mart heading out of town. Let's get some white T-shirts. I think six come in a pack or something."

I looked around and tried to figure out what else we could do. I prayed, "Lord, this may seem crazy to you, but we all want to be successful. Help us figure this out. Please."

Opening my eyes, I looked at Bea. Her pants looked weird. I saw a tag. So I asked, "Bea, what kind of pants are you wearing?"

"Girl, don't laugh. I'm wearing my pants inside out."

"Why?"

"That's what a Beta told me to do," Bea said.

"Then that's the ticket. It doesn't matter what kind of pants we have on—as long as they're inside out, they'll be uniform," I announced.

Twenty minutes later we arrived at the University of Southeastern Arkansas campus. My stomach dropped worse than when I was on the wildest amusement park ride. I only hoped we could stay on our game.

"We can't just walk into an empty building on campus like this," a girl, whose gold chain said Lanna, shouted out.

I smiled. "Yup. We can. Line up. Shortest to tallest. All the lines I saw last year were that way, so they would expect us to enter correctly."

There were twenty of us. I was number ten in the line. When we walked into the room we couldn't believe there were ten other girls from the host school lined up tight by height, all wearing nice black jogging suits. There had to be about sixty or seventy Betas scattered throughout. It was crazy. They even had scary music playing in the background, like we were in some horror flick. The Betas were practically salivating, ready to pledge our two lines together.

"You guys couldn't even be on time," Keisha said, moving close to us and looking scarier than a witch.

"I heard Keisha is the craziest of them all," Trisha said from in front of me.

"Who was that?" Bea was number eleven, so she was behind me.

Trisha said, "She's called the meanest Beta in the state of Arkansas. We're probably about to get our butts kicked tonight."

"Who told the fat girl to come in?" Keisha said, as she pulled Bea out of the line and punched her in her gut.

I couldn't believe I was just standing there and doing nothing. Bea was tough though. She didn't let out one moan.

"Oh, so that's not gonna do it. Then how about your whole line pay for me having to look at your bulging stomach? This T-shirt is too short." Keisha turned and looked at her sorority sisters. "Y'all, because I'm looking at her big self, um, I want a cake. I want to see which of these two lines can get me a cake first."

The other ten girls got together and headed for the door. "But before you guys can do anything, I want one hundred push-ups, one hundred sit-ups and one hundred jumping jacks from everybody."

We huddled together. The other group was starting their push-ups. Already we were behind.

"Sorry you guys, my fault. How we gonna do all this and beat them?" Bea said, looking down.

I tapped her on the back as I said, "Well, can anybody draw?"

Trisha raised her hand. She went to her jean backpack and pulled out a drawing pad and showed us all some clothes she sketched. She even had colored pencils. The rest of us were amazed.

I said, "Girl, you came ready. You're so good. Okay, draw the prettiest cake you can think of. We need to break up in groups. Some of us do push-ups, some do jumping jacks, while the rest do sit-ups. Let's put Trisha in the middle."

Fifteen minutes later, we were done. The other group had just left. Bea stood and went over to Keisha.

Keisha said, "What? You just gonna hand me something and not address me?"

Bea didn't look her in the eye. "What am I supposed to call you?"

"Big Sister Mean Machine," Keisha said, as she rolled her eyes and neck.

Bea said, "Big Sister Mean Machine, we've done our push-ups, our sit-ups and our jumping jacks, and here is your cake."

"Y'all may not be the coolest looking bunch, but y'all sure got sense," Keisha told us.

Edythe and Penelope, whom we hadn't seen the whole time we'd been in the place, came up to us and smiled. We heard the cheers from the Betas, who wore Alpha chapter emblems. The Betas from University of Southeastern Arkansas were upset at the poor performance of their line.

One Beta that was from the other school said, "Keisha, dog their tails out when they come back, embarrassing us like this. Give it to them."

Big Sister Mean Machine said, "Oh, you ain't got to worry. No scrub trying to get my letters will be shown up that easily. We just asked them to think. If they can't use their brains now, then I know they won't be able to use them later."

I was so terrified. What was she planning to do? Surely she was all talk and no action, right?

When the other girls came back with a cake from Publix, Keisha cut it and roughly stuffed a piece in each of their mouths, lightly pushing it back as far as it could go.

Suddenly, we heard coughing. Bea hit me and pointed at this girl that was having a tough time. The pledge started choking, and the Betas got scared. They just fled the room. Girls from her line swarmed around her. Some chick from my line started praying out loud. Trisha and Bea ran over and got water from a vending machine.

"I don't know if I want any part of this," Lanna called out.

The looks on all our faces reflected our horror and confusion. Cries and screams echoed from the room. I think we all knew we weren't supposed to be participating in this unsanctioned activity, and now we knew why. We were just starting this pledge stuff. How could the Betas just bail and leave someone choking? None of us were doctors. This was seriously brutal.

GIFT

"We've got to get Katie to a hospital and get her checked out," I said to all of the girls on the underground lines with me.

Everyone stepped back to give her room. Trisha got on her cell and tried to call 911. A girl on her line rushed over and knocked the cell out of Trisha's hand.

"No, no. We can't take her to a hospital," she said. "The Betas would get in trouble and we would never be able to be on line."

I wanted letters, but not at the expense of someone dying. This was insane. Trisha shoved the girl out of the way and picked up her phone, ready to make the call.

Thankfully, one of the girls on the University of Southeastern Arkansas line said she'd interned in a doctor's office. She thumped the choking girl on her back, and all of a sudden the girl started coughing instead of choking. What a relief!

"Yeah, I'm going to be fine," the girl said to us moments later as her line sisters looked after her. "You guys have blessed me. You just don't know. Thanks for not leaving me. I'm quitting this."

"Alright, well let's get out of here," Bea said to me. "Everyone from Western Smith round up. Let's go."

Though the girl was fine, I was dumbfounded at what had taken place. The Betas had left without knowing she was going to be okay. What was I signing myself up for?

I thought about Creed's bruises. I so hoped Creed wasn't experiencing any of this drama himself. I could only pray he was okay.

Trisha came over to me and said, "Come on, Hayden, let's get out of here."

"I know, but . . ."

"There's no buts—we have to get out of here, her line sisters got her," Trisha said as she grabbed my hand and we waved goodbye.

As soon as we stepped out of the building, it was darkness. I was so angry, if I had seen one of those Beta Gamma Pi girls, I might have had to stuff something down their throats myself. Then all of a sudden bright headlights were shining on us. The Betas hadn't left after all.

"What are we supposed to do?" one of the girls called out.

Bea said, "We're going to get in our cars and leave. Do them like they did us. When it all goes down they don't want to get their hands dirty. What kind of mess is that? Come on, y'all don't stop, don't stop."

But before we could get into our cars, Big Sister Keisha Mean Machine got out of her car and said, "I see you guys got some medical experience in your blood. Well, that's good. Since you're so crafty and can work everything out, I'm going to give you a present. We told you at the rush that your packets were due in a week. They better be to us in three days. See ya!"

She got into her car and left. Eight other cars sporting Beta Gamma Pi tags roared out of the parking lot one after another.

One girl said, "How am I going to get my packet together that quickly?"

Looking at our bewildered faces, most of us didn't know what we were going to do. The way the Betas had handled the trouble they created should have made us all nervous enough not to continue, but it seemed like we all wanted this so bad that no one was running to tell.

We all went back to Bea's place, since she lived alone, and started working on filling out the questionnaire. Most of my stuff was lined up. I had to have a recommendation letter from a Beta who had been active for three consecutive years; since my mom was the president of her chapter and pretty much knew every Beta in the state, I had all kinds of surrogate aunts willing to write my letter. I felt bad when some girls said they didn't know anybody. Betas weren't like any other sorority where you could call up a favor letter. No, they were real particular, especially the ladies from the alumnae chapter. If they didn't know you, they weren't writing anything for you. You also had to have a letter of recommendation from a public service organization.

Bea asked, "Hayden, you think the people you worked with will write mine?"

With a syrupy sweet expression, I shook my head. I took working in the community seriously. Whether I became a Beta or not, I wanted to give back. My roommates and I had been serving others all last year when we were freshman. Every Thursday after school we were at the local middle school working with at-risk girls. So getting my service letter wasn't an issue either. Since my grades were good, getting my transcript wasn't a problem.

Trisha said, "If I got the grades, I barely made it. I might have to get mine altered."

"I don't understand," I said to her.

"People do it all the time. They get somebody in the registrar's office to change a few grades to get their GPA up. I think I need higher than a 2.5."

I said, "Well, if 2.5 is the requirement then they should vote you in."

"What? Are you kidding me?" Bea cut in. "These girls are ruthless. They're looking for anything they can to eliminate us. Even if your packet is the best one they have seen, if they don't want you they'll find a way to kick you off." Even after knowing this, we all continued working on our packets late into the night.

The next evening, Creed and I went to the movies. When he called to see me, I had to take him up on it. Just being with him gave me comfort. I couldn't talk about what I'd been going through with anyone, but when he embraced me as we watched the flick, I could tell he understood.

"Hayden, you'll be okay," he leaned over and whispered in my ear. "Know that I think about you every day."

We were both exhausted, but the touching we did in the dark spoke a million words. The brother cared for me. And thankfully, the Pi's hadn't killed him.

When he dropped me off back at my place, the kiss he planted on my lips soothed my soul better than a cup of hot chamomile tea. I knew we wouldn't see each other often while pledging, but we put some gas in our tank of love to carry us for a while.

Five days after the horrific choking incident, I was sitting in front of thirty Betas for an interview. My mom had prepped me: "Wear a suit. Don't look too jazzy. Don't go in there with your face bland, throw on just a bit of makeup, smile after each question, but don't look too confident or cocky. Wear neutral colors, no red, no pink, no purple or blue."

My interview was going well. I answered five questions in a row. Every time one of them asked me something I was there, ready with the answer. But when the advisor stepped out of the room you would have thought a barracuda had just attacked me or something.

The President, Edythe, said, "So you just think that you are God's gift to the world? If you've got it going on so well, why do you want to be a Beta?"

"We don't want her," Big Sister Keisha Mean Machine screamed out.

Taking a deep breath, I said, "First of all, I do apologize if I have led you all to believe that I think I am all that. I consider myself a very humble person and I'd like to be a member of this organization because of the Betas that I have seen all last year. They were helping people who cannot help themselves, confident in running things within the Student Government Association and they have the best GPA on campus. I've had to strive hard to even be a part of this group, but if you make me a member, hopefully you will be confident that I won't bring you guys down. I'd just be a bonus to a group of girls who already have it going on."

"Alright now!" Penelope called out.

I saw them mumbling to each other. I guess I gave a pretty good answer. Now I just had to wait and see if I made their line.

"Well, Father," I prayed aloud, on my knees in my bedroom, "I know it's been a while since I've really talked to You. And if my mother knew I hadn't been to church all semester I'd certainly be in trouble with her as well. I know You've got to be disappointed and I am sorry about that. It's just school and this line, but You're God so You know. I haven't heard anything so I'm a little worried. I wanted to be a Beta, but like always I only want Your will for me. These last few weeks I have certainly seen another side of sorority life that I didn't even know existed, but I feel firmly from the depths of my soul that this is something that You support. After all, it is an organization founded on Christian principles. If I could just get in, I'd make sure that we get our business back in order. Please Lord, I so want to wear that lavender and turquoise. In Jesus' name . . ."

Before I said Amen, I heard screaming through the house as the front door closed. Somebody had great news. No matter what it was I was going to be supportive.

"What's going on?" I asked as I peeked outside of my door.

Chandra turned around and said, "Girl, it's Bridget and Myra. You know what just happened?"

"Yeah, Bridget must have made the MEM line and Myra must have made the Nu one."

I knew one had good news, but both, already. Chandra saw that it was a bittersweet moment for me. She came over and gave me a hug.

"You know we always girls, right? If them Betas don't select you it would be the stupidest thing they've ever done."

"Yeah," I told her, trying to sound like I had put it all in God's hands. "So far it's a no."

"Did you hear anything yet?" Bridget asked as she rushed over and showed me her letter from the MEMs national headquarters. "And look, it's even on silver and gold stationery."

"Is she okay?" I overheard Myra asking Chandra.

They were such great roommates. We were all doing our own individual thing, but we had a deep connection to each other. No one wanted to see the others not get what they longed for.

"It's no big deal. I know everybody is getting their information tonight. Before you ask again, I haven't gotten a call or a letter. So I probably didn't make the Beta line, but I'll be able to help you guys." I threw my arms around Bridget and Myra.

"Well, I'd like to stay and chat but I've got to go. You know I'm praying for you, Hayden. It's going to work out," Myra said, an overnight bag in her arms.

"Where you going?" Chandra asked, trying to get all of the scoop. "And I thought sororities didn't haze?"

"Now, I did not say that I was going to get hazed," Myra replied quickly.

Bridget said nothing, she just went into her room and packed as well.

"You want to go get some Chinese food?" Chandra asked me.

"Naw."

"Girl, you cannot stay in here and sulk. I will not have it. Pack your stuff up and let's go."

"Well, what if the Betas come looking for me or whatever?" I said, trying to be optimistic.

"If they want you they'll find you. Plus, you've got your cell phone, right?"

She had a point. I had been locked up in the house all day hoping, wishing and praying for some kind of letter saying I was on line. Why should I stay in all night sulking?

We went to our favorite Chinese spot and pigged out. An hour and a half later, I still had not received a phone call as we headed back to our place. As we reached the front door, lights flashed.

"What's that?" Chandra said, shielding her eyes from the blinding light.

I was already hip to the signal. Someone was here for me. I was scared to believe this could be good news.

"Go on in, Chandra. I think I made it," I told her as my heart raced.

"You sure you straight?"

"Yeah, bye girl." We hugged and I walked to the car where the light was coming from.

I knew not to tap on the window or anything and after about three minutes the door opened. I sighed in relief when I saw Penelope. She didn't say I made it and she looked kind of worried. She just handed me a piece of paper and got back into the car. It was the address for a nearby park. After searching through my purse for my keys, I jumped in my car and was there within minutes. As soon as I got there the lights were on me again and I saw a clear lighted path. I stepped on a lavender colored brick, as a chorus sang from the darkness.

"Congratulations Hayden, you're the last person to be on the Beta Gamma Pi line. Follow the lavender and turquoise lights to meet your line sisters," Edythe said.

The singing continued as I walked. It seemed so surreal, so sweet, so precious. My heart was calm and I forgot all the drama I had endured. I felt special being serenaded.

"You are now my sister, no longer just my friend, though you're just a baby Beta, we're connected till the end. I will show you the way, our bond will be great, now you will forever have Beta Gamma Pi on your mind. What a blessing you have made line."

As soon as they were finished singing, I was in a circle formed by a group of girls that I didn't know. These girls couldn't be my line sisters. All of the ladies who had been with me during all of the underground stuff were not around. I was hardly able to breathe, I was so excited, but completely devastated that my new-found friends that I had bonded with weren't with me.

Then I felt a touch and heard a familiar voice. "I'm here, girl," Bea said.

Trisha said, "Me too."

The three of us hugged so tight.

"Where is everybody else?" I said, hoping they were around the corner.

"We're the only three that made it," Trisha said, as the three of us hugged again. We had a bittersweet moment, crying tears of joy for ourselves. We also cried tears of sorrow for those who didn't make it. I didn't know why they weren't picked. I heard when you participate in underground lines, you're taking a chance to see if you'll actually make the real pledge line, but I never thought that rumor to be true. I guess I was wrong.

Bea said, "I guess we better count our blessings."

I had arrived at the park at one in the morning and I didn't leave until four AM. I was so tired. I did make it back to my apartment in one piece.

"Thank you, Lord," I said. "This is exactly what I prayed for and because You honored my request, I know this is going to be a good experience. Help me not to lose my mind on line. I love You, Lord. Thank You and I pray for all of those who didn't make it. May they keep on knowing that it'll be okay."

When I stepped out of the car, I heard a car honk. Now, I was a little nervous. Though our area was secure it was scarcely patrolled by college police. It was after four in the morning and the bushes that surrounded my path made the place look so dark. Who would be honking at me? I already knew the Betas put on their head-lights, so I knew it wasn't them. I walked a little briskly to my door, but then the honking started again and a car started moving in my direction.

"Wait, wait. It's me," the faint yet familiar voice called out through the window.

When the car got close enough, I noticed it was Creed's. "Hey you!"

"You seem alone," Creed said, looking all around the parking lot. "Hayden, I can't go to my place. Can I come in? I need to hide out."

"Yeah, just park your car way down there. I don't want anyone thinking you're at my house."

"Cool, I'll be right there."

I never let a guy into my apartment and I knew my dad would be totally angry if he knew I was entertaining a young man at four in the morning. But he was overseas fighting a war and we didn't exactly see eye to eye on everything. I was in college now, I had to do my thing. If Creed was out this late and couldn't go back to his place obviously he had good news, and I could tell him I made line too.

When he came through the front door, I wrapped my arms around his neck and my lips found their way to his. I was a little bummed out that he wasn't hugging me back. Then he put me down and pulled out a bouquet of lilies.

"These are the sorority's flower," I said.

"Yeah!"

"How'd you know?"

"You're not home at this hour of the night, and that

could only mean you're doing what the rest of us are—you're on somebody's line. Congratulations girl, I knew you'd make it."

"I didn't know I would. How many are on your line?" I asked him.

"Thirteen of us—and you?" he asked.

"It's sixteen."

"Cool."

"Come on." I pulled him into my bedroom. Thankfully, I had cleaned up since I was home all day long.

"So how did you feel when you found out?" he asked me.

"I don't know."

"What do you mean you don't know? I'm a little sore on my bottom, but I feel great," he teased, as he rubbed his butt.

"It's just most of the girls we were underground with didn't make line."

"That happens all of the time; everyone knows the risk you take. Supposedly the ones who didn't take part in any of the underground stuff are really going to get it when it really gets down to it, so they won't be paper. It should balance out. How many of y'all survived?"

"Only three."

"Dang, they were brutal. On my line, ten of us made it and we only have three new guys."

"See what I'm saying? How am I supposed to be happy when so many people who wanted this didn't get it? Why did they choose me?"

"Uh, because you're beautiful, smart, and you're fine

as I don't know what," Creed said, as he pulled my body toward his and we fell onto my bed.

"Okay, soooo you got to go home."

"I just told you I can't."

"What do you mean you can't?"

"They told us we can't go home for twenty-four hours. They took our keys. I'm sure they're staying there. I know when I get back I won't have a TV, a stereo, food, I might not even have books."

"Are you serious? Now how is that supposed to make you a better Pi?"

"To figure out how to survive, I guess. I don't know if all of this stuff is supposed to have some kind of subliminal message to make us better for the organization. Half of it is stupid, but I'm excited to go through the process, you know?"

"But I can't have some boy in my crib, in the middle of the night, in my bed with me. No."

"I'm not just some boy, how about I'm your boyfriend."

"Says who?"

"Says the girl that is going to say yes. You are going to have to help me get through this. These guys are crazy and I need to have something special, someone awesome, and someone all mine. I need to be thinking of you."

So very excited, I nodded, yes.

He kissed my neck and went to my ear. If I hadn't been lying down I would have fallen. I was so mesmerized by his touch. Tired in each other's arms we lay still.

"You're gorgeous and you're mine," Creed said, as we drifted off to sleep. "What a gift!"

PROMISE

After a week of underground hell, I was excited to take my first official step into Beta Gamma Pi. It was the Pi induction ceremony. I still didn't really know a lot of folks on my line. We had been doing things independently for all of our big sisters, chauffeuring them around, running errands, and doing everybody else's homework and research papers. It was a hot mess, but I wasn't quitting.

"So, we're really gonna do this?" Trisha turned around and said to me as the sixteen of us stood in line in our black dresses waiting to be escorted into the newly renovated theatre on campus for the ceremony.

I didn't know a lot about everybody on the line, but I did know a few things. Like the tallest girl, Audria, was from Alabama. The girl was a big religious person. Trisha and Bea thought she was a little fake and phony with it. Every time we saw her she lifted up her hands to the sky and proclaimed, "Praise the Lord." I was down with G-O-D myself, but I had to admit to my two girls that she was over the top.

"Y'all, I think we should pray," Audria shouted from the back.

"Why don't you just pray quietly for us," Bea said sarcastically, and half of the line snickered.

"We all need Jesus, Bea," Audria responded, a little put-off that everyone was mocking her.

"Don't hurt her feelings, Bea," I said over my shoulder as I lightly spanked Bea's big thigh.

"Watch it now! She's really gonna have to pray for you if you hit me again," Bea teased.

"Y'all two stop," Trisha said.

"Seriously Bea, we're about to go in here for this induction ceremony. The first official step into the sorority. This event should tug at our hearts. How better to get in the right spirit than by seeking God. What's wrong with getting a cool word?" I said, knowing a covering from up above would be a great thing.

"Aight Audria, say something for all of us," Bea said, relenting.

"Don't worry about it. I already did," Audria retorted.

"Well, forget it then," Bea said to her.

Then there was our number one, Dena, the shortest girl on our line. She was so shy. I wished she was a little tougher.

"Miss Dena over there is shaking," Trisha said to Bea and me.

Bea said, "See, I don't know how we gonna make it with the big sisters with one as weak as her. They shoulda took that other girl we had. Dang!"

"Yeah," Trisha agreed.

"I'm still really upset that my friend didn't make it. With the exception of you two, she's got all these girls beat, hands down. She had the grades, yet they took her through all those hoops and stuff for nothing," Bea lamented.

Then the girl in front of Trisha turned around, put her hands on her hips and said to the three of us, "Why are you guys griping about who is not here on this line? I tried to stay out of your conversation because I know you aren't talking to me, but I know I speak for everybody on this line when I say enough already. Contrary to what you think, the rest of us can carry our own. That's why we did make the line and your friends didn't. My name is Sharon. Don't you forget it."

Trisha wanted to take her hand and bash the girl when she turned back around, but I held her and said, "Just let it go."

Thankfully Penelope came and got us and escorted our line into the assembly. All the hostility that had been penned up in the waiting room was released when I walked into the room filled with Betas wearing white. The night before, Edythe told us to wear black for the ceremony. They told us the black we were wearing symbolized the darkness we were in before being connected to the Beta Gamma Pi light. When I passed my mom and saw the tears fall from her eyes, I knew this was a special ceremony. Though she wasn't forcing this on me, I knew it was something she really wanted for me. Something we would now be able to share. Something dear to her heart. Her sorority would soon be dear to mine for life.

Our initiation ceremony was breathtaking. With the

marble floor, crystal chandelier hanging from the ceiling, and the many mahogany chairs, I couldn't help but feel spellbound by the room's captivating beauty. The hundreds of small flickering lavender and turquoise candles all over the room symbolized our connection with the Beta Gamma Pi light. The chandelier lights were fairly dim, perhaps to allude to our darkness before coming into our newfound sisterhood. The room's center held a life-sized framed portrait of our five great founders. A hundred sunrise lavender and sunset turquoise sprayed flowers surrounded the base of the portrait. This was the moment I had dreamed of.

The ceremony lasted an hour, but it was so impactful. Every single thing the speakers said was so important and moving that it made me want to get up out of my seat and lead a nation. Before our induction was official they called each of us up individually to come sit in a royal chair, fit for a queen. It was there that we recited an eight-line pledge, confessing from the bottom of our soul that we were ready to pledge our vows. I knew that the vow to be a Beta was a serious commitment. I said every word with real passion for the sorority.

My mom then came up and put the Pi pin close to my heart. She leaned over and whispered in my ear that I would get the full letters upon completion of the whole pledge process. Though I couldn't wait for that moment, I took time to relish this special one.

With pride, she said, "I love you, Hayden. Enjoy this experience. When done the right way, it can change you and shape you for greatness."

As soon as the ceremony was officially over and we

were in the hall, there was a nice spread of food, mostly pies, symbolizing the Pi ceremony. Suddenly an irate Beta, who turned out to be Sharon's mom, came rushing up to our advisor.

"I'll tell you what, something funny is going on with these girls. My daughter can't even keep her eyes open. Most of this line was sleeping during the whole ceremony. If some hazing is going on, I will stop all this madness and take everybody's letters. You better hear me up in here. Touch my daughter and Alpha chapter will be no more."

Everyone froze. Sharon was just like her mom, and I didn't know if that was a good thing, but I certainly hoped the undergrad Betas heard what her mom was saying. I certainly didn't want to lose my letters before I even got them.

That same night, the sixteen of us were crammed into Big Sister Keisha Mean Machine's apartment. It must have been the smallest apartment in the city—and the oldest. Within the apartment, there were power strips everywhere to make up for the lack of outlets in the place. Alongside that eyesore there was an abundance of old looking furniture and stacks of dusty books. Twenty other Betas were surrounding Keisha, but they weren't familiar—and there weren't that many Betas on campus.

"I know some of these girls have graduated," Bea said to me.

Edythe went over to Keisha and said, "Look, we can't do any of this anymore. Did you hear what Sharon's mother said today? I'm not getting my letters taken because of you, Keisha. This is over the top."

"Whatever, I am not about to let these girls walk up in my sorority and not get a thorough pledge experience on my watch. They gotta pay dues just like everybody else. Where is the line president?"

We all stood still. What was a line president? Penelope hadn't told us about that.

"These dummies hadn't even selected a leader to answer for them. Maybe they need some cake shoved down their mouths."

Edythe saw us looking angry and confused. "Girls, as soon as you can, select someone that will represent you to all of us."

Keisha said, "Well, first just tell me whose momma said that stuff earlier today anyway?"

Nobody raised their hand. I didn't know Sharon, but I surely would not want to ask for trouble. However, as Big Sister Mean Machine started cussing, I knew anything but Heaven was about to break loose if someone didn't come clean.

Spitting and shouting, Keisha said, "Didn't y'all hear me, scrubs? I said whose momma said that anyway?"

All of us raised our hands. Instincts about protecting ourselves and our sisters kicked in all at once. I was proud to stand with a group of girls who cared more about the line than themselves.

"Y'all don't have to do that," Sharon turned around and said to us, "Big Sister Keisha Mean Machine, it was my mom."

Keisha went over and yanked Sharon out of the line. "Ha ha, I thought it was you. What yo' momma say? Nobody better not lay a hand on you?"

Keisha pulled Sharon's hair. She kicked her in the thigh. Then she shoved Sharon into all of her sorors.

"Keisha, I'm serious," Edythe said, helping Sharon to her feet.

Keisha went over and grabbed Sharon again, shoving Edythe out of the way. "Your mom said don't touch you, huh?"

We were all stunned when Keisha back-slapped her. Penelope went to stand in front of Keisha. The two of them stared each other down.

Finally Penelope said, "Hey, this is a little too much. I'm with Edythe, I don't want to get my letters removed."

"I knew I shouldn't have put the two of you guys in leadership. Y'all so weak. No backbone. Everybody knows you don't threaten a Beta and expect to get away with it. Just because of you, Sharon, this whole line is gonna catch it."

For the next hour, we scrubbed the two toilets and bathtubs. Some of us cleaned the kitchen and the rest of us wiped the windows and blinds. We were working swiftly, thinking the faster we got the task done the quicker we could get out of there and study.

Out of nowhere, Keisha came up to Bea and said, "I'm sick and tired of looking at you, fat girl. I told them not to put you on the line either. Sharon, where are you? You think your line sister is fat?"

Sharon said, "No, Big Sister Keisha Mean Machine."

"Okay, well give me a push-up. Now Bea, get on her back."

"I don't think I can hold her, Big Sister Keisha Mean Machine."

"Well, you shouldn't have said she wasn't fat. You said she wasn't, so you gonna hold her for five minutes. Go."

I said to Trisha, "Let's go, we can help."

"How?" Trisha said.

I moved over to the action and said, "She said she's got to hold her, well we can help hold her, too."

I got down on my back and Trisha got on the other side of Sharon. We allowed Bea to put her feet on us and that helped to prop her up.

"Oh, so y'all think y'all can outsmart me, huh? Edythe," she called out, "I want y'all to address her as Big Sister Dr. Edythe Right. Why? Because she's president and is always right to y'all. No one gives her orders. Y'all got it?"

"Yes ma'am," we said.

"Five minutes is up, Big Sister Dr. Edythe Right," I said.

"Naw, let them go longer," Keisha snapped. "Since they got help, ten minutes."

Then she went over to Bea and messed with her stomach. "Fatso, I'ma get that meat off of you if it's the last thing I do. We can't have no wobbly Betas."

"I'm bored," another Beta hollered out.

"Let me get you some entertainment," Keisha said to her. "Alright y'all, fall in line. We want to see a skit about domestic violence. Go. Now."

The four of us started scrambling toward the rest of our line sisters. Then all sixteen of us tried to come up with something. Keisha took a lamp and threw it at us. It cut Dena.

"That's what I'm talkin' about. I want to see one that is more real. Hit somebody, kick somebody. Do something."

The next thing you know Dena turned around and punched her number two. Hands were all out of control. We were beating each other up. You woulda thought it was a lady's boxing ring match, but the Betas were laughing and we looked like fools. What did this have to do with sisterhood and friendship? Absolutely nothing. The look on Edythe and Penelope's faces showed it, but they were in the minority. The rest of the girls in the chapter, and the old heads that had graduated already, who came back to grill us, were loving the discord.

Why did we stay? I wondered as I participated in the madness. Deep in my heart I believed in the sorority's core values. I was doing this for my mom's honor. And though I knew if she saw this she'd have my head herself, I *had* to stand and take it all. I was convinced this was the only way.

Penelope got up and said, "Alright, you guys, this is enough. That girl's got a bloody nose."

Keisha got up in her face and said, "I have had pints of blood drawn from pledges before, but I haven't paddled a soul. Relax, nobody has drank any rubbing alcohol. If you stop any of this small stuff we are doing with them, I guarantee you your little line will be paper."

Keisha moved out of the way and sat down. Penelope looked discouraged, but didn't respond. We were on our own now.

At three-thirty in the morning we were released from Keisha's apartment. We weren't allowed to park in front just in case some chapter advisor or someone that we knew came by. There could not be anything that appeared to connect us with Keisha. So we dashed around the back of her place to the two cars the sixteen of us had to pile into.

However, before we opened either car door, all kinds of emotions started coming from our group. Girls were screaming from pain, crying because they were scared, shouts of anger rang out. It was chaos.

Sharon keeled over, held her stomach and said, "I got to quit right now. I can't take any more of this."

Two or three girls stood behind her and nodded their heads in agreement. We all looked tore up, with bloody noses, and ripped up clothes. Who could blame anyone not wanting to keep the madness going.

Trisha got up in their faces and said, "What are y'all talkin' about quitting? What y'all think this was? See, that is why I don't understand why they put folks on the line who didn't go through any pre-underground stuff. Obviously these folks ain't tested. They can't take it. This is crap, the line might get dropped because of weakness."

Bea stood behind her and nodded. I understood her argument, but she was tripping. I knew there were no limits to hazing, but I just never fathomed that girls who would soon be my sisters could be so cruel.

"Look, if you think I signed up to be beaten up, or to fight with y'all, then you can have this crazy, stupid sorority," Sharon ranted.

Audria, visibly shaken, agreed. "This is supposed to be a Christian organization and God doesn't like brutality. They are doing this all wrong. Obviously, with what just happened tonight, we can't stop them. Us hitting on each other was their entertainment for the night. God isn't pleased with none of what took place."

"Stop with the God stuff," Trisha said to her.

Bea said, "God gives us free will to choose, okay. But you heard Keisha. We could be paper if we don't go through a little something."

Dena came over and said, "Excuse me, excuse me, if I could just say one thing."

Everybody looked at her expectantly, but when she had all sixteen of us ready to listen she froze. It took a minute, but Dena was finally able to speak her piece, "Well, if we could all stick together, I think we could get them to not go to the extreme on everything. Ultimately, they don't want to lose the line."

After all that wait, no one listened to her. Trisha and Bea started arguing with Sharon and Audria. I just felt so overwhelmed.

"Guys, we don't need to listen to this. We don't need to stand here and fuss," Sharon said, as she appealed to the majority. "Look at us, blood dripping, arms bruised. I don't know about you guys, but my ribs are hurting. Come on, let's go back to the house and tell them we quit."

Bea stood between them all. "I wish y'all would. But you can't, if you gonna drop line, you need to turn in an official letter to the advisor. We signed a document stating that. You are not going back to that house. You are not going to make it worse on the rest of us."

Sharon said, "I can't believe you gonna stand there and tell me what I can and cannot do. I put up with this for far too long from them girls up there thinking they can push me around. You might be triple my size, Bea, and I might have had to carry you on my back all night long, but I am not gonna take any more junk from you."

Bea started taking off her earrings. "I know she didn't talk about my size. It's on now, whatever, come on, Sharon."

"Trisha, get your friend," Sharon said.

"I'm not getting her at all," Trish replied, almost wanting another fight to take place. "Bea's got a point—I don't want you all messing it up for the rest of us. We tried to tell you. They put the wrong girls on line. Most of the ones who had the heart to endure it all were part of the pre-underground . . ." Trisha said, turning to everyone.

"Yeah, we know. See, we always have to hear that from y'all," Sharon said, with watery eyes. "Thinking that you guys are the only ones who deserve to be Betas, just because you can take a punch or two, you're better than us. We have morals. We have standards and we are not going to take it anymore. *We* are actually true Beta material. You signed some form saying you wouldn't participate in hazing, yet you been involved in being hazed all along. All we got to do is turn you guys in and we could be Betas without you all anyway. At least we were actually on an official line recognized by headquarters before we participated in any of these activities."

I never even thought of that. They had a point, but I still didn't want them to mess it up for me. This was extreme what we were going through. There might have been lines that have had it worse, but we had true blood, sweat, and tears to prove that what they were doing to us was wrong.

"Come on, y'all," Sharon said to all the other girls. "Let's go tell them we aren't taking this anymore."

Trisha hit me on the arm. "Do something."

I just stood there. What could I do?

Bea went around and got in Sharon's face one last time. She yanked Sharon's sore arm. "I'ma tell you right now, you go up those stairs, it's gonna be on. I promise."

BLESSED

Thinking from the depths of my soul, I ran in between Bea and Sharon and just started praying aloud. "Lord, this is crazy. We are at each others' throats when we should be coming together. It's going to take everything we have to make this line. Help us to say the right words to each other. Help us to put You first. Deep down I know we all wanted this so we can give back. Though our actions and attitudes right now aren't reflecting that, I know if we give all this to You—all of the craziness, the madness, the anger, the hurt, and the pain—You and only You can make it better. In Jesus' name I pray. Amen."

I didn't know who was with me or who wasn't, but I felt a peace come over us when I heard fifteen other Amens. This was emotional for us all. We'd been physically and emotionally beat up on. Though we were one line, we were made up of sixteen uniquely strong people. Obviously, we all handled the stress differently. However, at that moment we needed to act as one. We had to come to a unanimous decision. What one did would affect us all.

Audria came up to me and said, "That was awesome. If Bea or Sharon don't have any objection, I think you need to be our line president."

I was stunned. That was the last thing I was expecting anybody to say to me. I just knew that none of us needed to quit. None of us needed to walk away. This was all-important to each of us for various reasons. And regardless of what anybody thought of my prayer, I had to take a stand because I knew the only One who could fix the drama, and it wasn't those crazy Betas who had been giving us hell.

"Alright, alright," Bea said, nodding. "I agree. Hayden would make an excellent line president."

Audria said, "Sharon, you cool with it?"

"I just don't know if I want to stay on this line," Sharon said, holding her gut. The anguish she felt earlier hadn't gone away yet.

I went over and gave her both my hands. "We don't know each other well and I'm sure you've got a lot of ill thoughts about me, but I do care about everyone."

"Well, I don't like how you've been talking about me with your friends, like I can't hear you guys. I'm right in front of you and Trisha," Sharon explained.

"Well, you're right. And I personally owe you an apology for that. But Trisha, Bea, and I went through a lot before you guys came. And though we shouldn't hold that against y'all, it just seemed a little unfair. And now for y'all to be talking about throwing in the towel and turning us in for something we participated in—it's just a lot, and it certainly makes tempers flare," I said in the calmest voice I could muster.

"You're right. I shouldn't have threatened to just spoil what y'all have going on because I want to be done," Sharon admitted.

"We've got to find a way to be smarter though. What I admire about you, Sharon, is that you won't take crap from anybody. None of us should have to. I want those three letters so bad, but am I willing to die for them? Not at all, and tonight really got me. I've been listening to you all go back and forth, but truth is, I also need to reevaluate what I'm trying to be a part of. I guess I've been telling myself that once I became a Beta, I could change a lot of the foolishness that goes along with pledging. I mean if the national president had any idea of what was going on . . ."

"So we should tell somebody. I mean why are we putting up with this?" Sharon said.

"Because I know I have something to give and I know you do too. You have so much heart, Sharon, yet you're also tough. That's something we don't want to lose. We're all completely different, but it takes us all to be a line."

Audria chimed in, "Can't we figure out a way to outsmart them?"

"Yeah," Trisha said, "like when they wanted Sharon to put Bea on her back. It was your brilliant idea, Hayden, for us to kneel down and take some of the pressure off."

"We just got to keep thinking like that, guys. We can do it. We can't let these girls win. They're about to graduate. Let's change the image and the focus of the Betas from what it is now to what it was when the founders gave their all to start it. We can be the difference together," I said.

I put out my hand. Then fifteen other hands piled on top of mine. Because we put God in the middle, He helped us find a way to work it out.

There I stood among my peers, each of them looking toward me for answers. I didn't take the leadership position lightly. I was honored that they wanted me to represent them. Though I knew even the greatest leader probably gets a little apprehensive at times during a crisis, there was no time to falter. I had to be strong, be ready, and willing to stand up for the group.

"You guys go home. I'm gonna go and get Penelope and talk to her," I uttered.

"You can't talk to her by yourself!" Sharon called out. "You know she is foolish."

"It's not just her that's crazy," Trisha said. "All the rest of those Betas are cuckoo too. We're not gonna let you go in there by yourself."

Though I appreciated their support, I felt strong enough going alone. So I picked up my cell phone and without hesitation I dialed Penelope's number.

I was surprised when on the first ring, she said, "Hello."

I could hear all the other Betas in the background. At that moment I was intimidated. What was I thinking calling her?

"Hayden, this is your number. Are you there? Is anybody there?" Penelope called out.

Snapping back into reality, I uttered, "Yeah, yeah I'm here. I need to see you alone. It's important."

"We were just talking about you guys. Is everybody okay?" Penelope said, so low it sounded like she was whispering.

"It's pretty severe. Can you please meet me alone? The status of the line depends on it," I said, looking around at the bleak faces of my line sisters.

"Okay, okay. I'll be right there," Penelope said, as we set up the details of where we were going to meet.

"Do you trust her?" Bea said to me.

"I do. Let me handle this, guys. Y'all go home."

I inhaled as I walked to my car. We'd dogged disaster. We had to keep it that way, so I headed to meet the leader of the line.

Penelope kept her word and came alone to the designated meeting spot, the nearby Waffle House. I was sitting inside with a cup of hot chocolate.

"Can I get you something?" I said to her when she first sat down.

"No, I want to make this as quick as possible. It's late and you don't need to be out here alone. What's going on?"

"The line is in jeopardy," I said defiantly.

"I really don't understand. Talk to me, Hayden. What's up?"

There was no need beating around the bush. I just wanted to get it all out and see what she was going to say.

"A lot of the girls want to quit. This has been a lot. We've had bloody noses, bruises, all kinds of stuff. We didn't sign up for this, Penelope. Some are mad because they were on the pre-underground line and felt like they proved themselves and shouldn't have to endure the brutality. Others who didn't go through that, feel like they never let you guys think they would stand for such craziness. We're divided and some want to squeal to the chapter advisor."

Penelope looked at me with seriousness at that moment. She knew if someone blew the whistle she'd be held responsible. She had to fix this.

"Penelope, I know you tried to stand up against some of the other Betas, but they shot you down cold. I just don't know if we can take it anymore." I sipped on the hot chocolate and waited for her response.

"So who are you supposed to be?" she said smartly.

I really didn't understand where the hostility was coming from because I came to her from the heart. I thought we were cooler than this, but she quickly let me know that in her mind I was still a pledge. How dare I tell her they needed to change or we'd walk away. But that's what I said and I was waiting for a response.

"Okay, so you're not gonna answer me?" she asked.

"I'm line president," I told her as my neck happened to roll, further making the point that I could speak for everyone.

"Oh my gosh!" she said excitedly, as she got up and gave me the biggest hug. "They chose you to be the leader? Do you know how hard it is to get girls to agree on one person and they chose you already? Oh wow, this is major! They sent you here to talk to me? I'm loving it. I'm so proud of you, Hayden."

Okay, I didn't know where all of that was coming from. After she'd been distant, now she was being nice to me. It didn't matter, I was here for one reason—to get her to call off the wolves.

"You just work your girls. Tell them Edythe and I got this. It's not going to be easy, but we'll certainly get the sisters to back down some. I'm so proud of you. This is a blessing. You're the line president! Alright girl, keep working what you got. But I've got to go, we can't be seen together." Then Penelope got up and jetted.

I guess I had made her aware that she needed to get her girls to back off. I hoped she could change things. If she didn't, me and my line sisters would take action. Whatever that meant. I sure hoped Penelope could fix things.

The next two nights, we didn't have any underground activity. It was so awesome for us all to be in the library catching up on our studying. My line sisters were praising me for setting the Betas straight.

"I don't know what you said to them," Bea said to me as we sat together going over a psychology assignment. "But you did it."

"She is the girl! She is the woman! She is the queen!" Trisha got up from her seat and started bowing.

"Oh see, now you are tripping. Stop," I said, laughing.

"Well, we better get over there. We've got a gem ceremony tonight."

"Yeah, I'm so excited," Bea said.

"Me too!" I told the two of them. "I guess it's another step. Forget the hazing, this is what the national chapter says we should go through to be in this sorority. If we listen to every word they say to us, really take in the experience, I know we'll come out way better."

"You all caught up in this ceremony stuff," Bea said to me.

"Because I really want to be a Beta. I really want to understand what it's all about. How can I use this to make a difference if I don't have the proper training? That's like going into the science test and thinking we're going to get an A without studying! Uh uh! It don't work like that, my sisters," I said to them.

"Alright, alright. I see what you're saying," Trisha said.

We all went our separate ways and met up an hour later at the gem ceremony. It was the first of five sacraments we'd attend to get a deeper understanding of the beliefs and values of the organization. The event was in the same lovely theatre where we became initiates. I was overjoyed to move a step closer to my beloved Beta Gamma Pi.

Edythe was at the mic with the advisor. They started singing the Gamma hymn. It's the song for pledges. As we walked in, Edythe said, "Tonight is the first gem ceremony. You'll be going through a life altering experience. This gem, a ruby, represents leadership. We know that deep inside each Beta is a powerful woman ready to take the world by storm."

Then the advisor took the mic and said, "A leader never steps back from any adversity in front of her. Leaders stand boldly. Always upholding justice. You speak for those who can't speak for themselves and you also speak for those who depend on your strength."

Penelope came over and directed us all up to the stage. There were different cards with quotes on them that embodied principles of leadership which we read aloud. At the end, Edythe stood with a sword and said, "With this sword, I deem you a leader of strength."

Then we read a card that said, "And I accept the honor. I will not let Beta Gamma Pi down. I will be a leader with purpose, vision, and passion."

Then Edythe knighted us with the sword.

The ceremony was so powerful and impactful. I'd made a pledge to lead my generation to greatness.

After, we each held a red candle symbolizing strength and sang the meaningful Gamma hymn. Then there was a prayer and we exited the ceremony. I always thought being a leader was a part of my duty, but being in this room, with this group, at this time, I felt that leadership was truly in my blood, in my soul, and in my heart.

Anyone can go about their life caring only about themselves, doing their own thing, and standing up for nothing. But a person of substance, quality, and stamina is someone who wants to make the world better through change. Feeling that, knowing that, going through that, made this gem ceremony extra special for me. I didn't know what was next to come, but I knew I was a leader. God called me to stand for Him. Believing that and being empowered by that made me feel blessed.

GONE

$\mathcal{P}$enelope found a way to evade her line sisters and keep our line happy at the same time. One of the requirements for becoming a Beta was passing a comprehensive test covering the history, purpose and mission of the sorority. She had given us an impromptu practice test and all sixteen of us had failed it. This was harder than any college exam I had ever taken. The three-hour exam was comprised of multiple choice, matching and fill-in-the-blank questions, and an essay section.

We received a Beta Gamma Pi manual at the beginning of the process. We were supposed to know it front to back, which was virtually impossible without adequate study time, and if we had to do this underground foolishness there was no way we could study that and finish our school work. So for the last four days, Edythe, the Chapter President, and Penelope, the Vice President and leader of the line, kept us away from their sorors who wanted desperately to distract us.

"You guys hurry up. Get inside," Penelope said, as we got to a new location none of the Betas knew about. "Nobody followed y'all, did they?"

"No, nobody followed us. We checked," I assured her.

Edythe asked, "Because they're getting real antsy. You sure nobody followed you?"

"No, nobody was following us," Bea confirmed.

We all sat down and pulled out the manuals to begin studying. But then Dena started rustling around, looking for something. No one could concentrate.

Dena got up and said, "Aw, I left my manual in the car."

Before Penelope could stop her, she fled outside. Suddenly, all craziness broke loose when Big Sister Keisha Mean Machine stood in the doorway with ten other not-so-happy Betas.

"Edythe and Penelope, I need to speak to you right now," Keisha hollered out.

We were scattered all over the room. Instinctively, we dropped our pens and books and fell in line. Second nature was in and logic was obviously out.

"Yeah, y'all better get up and show some respect," Keisha said to us with a mean stare that scared me. "Penelope, I thought you knew where they were, girl. I've been calling you. You won't answer your phone. Stupid little pledges can't even think for themselves. We were following them, but were lagging so far back that we lost them until one of your girls came outside. Just dumb! Obviously they want a butt whipping."

Sharon was in front of Trisha, her regular spot, and she said, "Y'all, if they touch me, I'm out of here."

"Just hold it together," I said. "Ain't nobody gonna have to go nowhere."

"Is Penelope going to handle this?" Bea said from behind me.

"We wouldn't be hiding out in the first place if she was able to tell Keisha what part of her body to kiss and mean it," Trisha said.

"Just stay cool, guys," I said.

"I don't understand the two of y'all," Keisha said as she pulled Penelope and Edythe to her face. "Y'all supposed to want what's best for the sorority, not stand up for these little hussies."

"You went too far last time, Keisha," Edythe said, surprising us all by standing up for us.

"Girl, get out of my way," Keisha said, pushing her to the side. "Bring in the stuff, y'all."

One of the old heads said, "Yeah, we got it right here."

"See, pledges, we figured you guys were studying so hard that y'all were hungry. Now it's time to eat a Beta sandwich. You jerks have a minute to get rid of these peanut butter and jelly sandwiches. I don't know how you're going to do it, but you better make sure that everyone has some."

"They don't have time to do this." Penelope snatched the bread as Keisha tried to hand it to Dena at the front of the line. "They're studying. They have an exam to take. Or they won't be Betas at all."

"Whatever girl, please, that is not as important as them passing *my* exam. This is Alpha Chapter. We have history here that cannot be ignored. Everybody has to eat the Beta sandwich in a minute and this line is no exception. Y'all don't even want to know what the consequences are if you don't comply."

"I'm allergic to peanuts," Sharon wailed, surprising us all.

What a good idea, I thought. Three more girls on the line said they were allergic as well. Keisha looked as if she wasn't having it.

Then Sharon started shaking and said, "No, I'm serious."

Trisha said, "Did you hear that, Hayden? Tell them that she is allergic for real."

I raised my hand. Sharon wasn't a kidder. If she was allergic, Keisha needed to back off.

"What?" Keisha responded, looking like she wanted to throw the peanut butter and jelly at me.

"Sharon really is allergic to peanuts, Big Sister Keisha Mean Machine."

"That's a cop-out. I don't believe you guys. Now hush up and get ready to eat this. You all do not want a beatdown. Go!" she said, as everybody except Sharon started scrambling over to the peanut butter.

There wasn't even a knife. We had to use our fingers to put the peanut butter and jelly on the bread.

"Just don't eat any," I said to Sharon. "Fake it. Make it look like you are."

"Okay, okay. I can do that. But I can't touch the stuff," Sharon said.

Unfortunately, Keisha and the rest of the Betas were watching every move we made. Keisha went over to Sharon with a sandwich and stuffed it in her mouth before any of us could stop her. *What had she done?*

"Chew it, darn it. Telling me you're allergic. I don't have time for that foolishness," Keisha said, as she shoved the remaining bread into Sharon's mouth.

Within an instant Sharon started choking. Her lips turned bright red and several bumps appeared on her face. She fell to the ground and no one else in the abandoned building moved. This was far worse than the girl who had choked. Sharon lay still. We were going to lose her.

"We've got to call the paramedics," Dena shouted.

None of us had cell phones except the leader of our line. The Betas always collected our phones so we wouldn't be disturbed while on line. Dena was right. We needed help immediately.

"Whatever, stand back," Keisha said. "Give her a second. No one is calling the paramedics. That's out."

Sharon was already a light-skinned girl but now she was deathly pale. Something was severely wrong and there was no way her fifteen line sisters were going to let her die on our watch.

Without caring about the consequences, I got up from Sharon's side and went to Penelope and said, "Give me your phone. NOW!"

Penelope hesitated for a minute. I didn't know Trisha and Dena were behind me. None of us were playing.

"You heard her," little Dena said, coming to my side.

"God don't like ugly," Audria shouted out.

I leaned over to Penelope and said, "If something happens to her I'll testify in court. Give me the phone."

Quickly, she reached into her pocket and handed it to me. I dialed 911 and gave them all of the information. Audria knelt down to take care of Sharon. Bea and the rest of the girls on the line started crying and praying.

"She can't breathe. She doesn't have air. Tell the paramedics to hurry, they've got to hurry," I said to the operator. "It might take them too long to get here. We need to get her into the car and get her to the hospital now."

Without worrying about what any Beta thought, we tended to our girl. I couldn't believe this was happening. Was not being a paper line so important that intelligent young women would threaten another woman's life?

When we got to the car, Penelope said, "Just stay on the phone with the operator. When you get to the emergency room, please call Edythe and let us know that Sharon's okay. Edythe's number is stored in my phone, but I can't go with you, I need to stay here."

Keisha came out of the door and said, "Y'all are letting them go to the hospital? This line is over."

"Well, if you wouldn't have come here, then this would have never started," Edythe turned to her and said.

I got in the driver's seat and Trisha sat beside me. In the back were Audria, Bea and Dena holding Sharon the best they could. I had driven fast before, but never as if I were trying to win the Indy 500 or something. Trisha looked out to my left and right when we got to stoplights. When she told me it was clear, I kept on going. We couldn't lose Sharon.

When I pulled up to the emergency door, Trisha ran to get help. Audria had Sharon's head in her lap and she was praying. All of us were glad she had such a strong connection with God. He had to help us.

"It's all my fault," I said, with my head on the steering wheel. "Sharon wanted to quit. She wanted to get out. I told her it was going to be okay. I thought we had it settled. She wouldn't be going through this if I hadn't talked her out of it."

Bea stroked the back of my head and said, "Like you can blame yourself. This is Keisha's fault. She came over and stuffed a peanut butter sandwich in someone's face, when they said they were allergic to it. I mean, even if she didn't believe Sharon, how could she take that chance? They need to lock her tail up in jail somewhere."

It seemed like it was taking Trisha forever to come back with help. Sharon's body had no movement. So we opened the door and carried Sharon in.

Bea screamed, "Somebody has to see her now! Help her now! We called on the phone, we spoke with the operator. HELP!"

"Okay, okay. We're here," one of the nurses said, as a doctor followed right behind her.

"She's critical! Let's take her back," the doctor said after checking her pupils.

Her face was so distorted, she clearly was allergic to peanuts in the worst way. All of us stayed around in the waiting room and held hands, praying. I had wanted to be a Beta more than anything these last few months, but if it meant losing Sharon, I would trade that dream for her being okay. Penelope's phone rang. I hadn't even realized that it was still in my hand.

"Hello," I answered.

"Hey, this is Edythe. How's Sharon? Please tell us that she is okay?"

"We don't know anything right now. She's in with the doctor," I said half-heartedly, not wanting to talk to any of them.

"Well look, we called Cynthia Berry, our advisor, and she is going to meet all of you at the hospital. If you don't want the line to drop, please be smart about what you tell her," Edythe said.

"Edythe, are you kidding me? Sharon is fighting for her life, and you're telling me to watch what I say to the advisor? I'm sorry, I can't even talk to you right now." I hung up the phone.

Tears started streaming down my face. I really needed to know how Sharon was doing. She had to be alright.

"Okay, what did Edythe want?" Bea said, breaking through my tears.

"Our advisor is going to be here in a second and Edythe wanted me to lie to her about what happened with Sharon."

"Wait!" Bea said. "Edythe has a point. We'll lose everything we worked so hard for if we tell the truth. Why don't we think about this?"

I could have smacked her as well. This had gone too far, we couldn't keep this under wraps. I just walked away, before I did or said anything I would regret.

"Hayden, did you hear me? We need to get our stories straight. We've gone through too much work for it to end now and have nothing to show for it," Bea said.

Trisha came over to rub my back. She wiped away a few of my tears but that didn't stop more from streaming down. How could wanting to be a part of a public service organization go so wrong?

"I know this is hard to think about right now, and I

know you don't want to hear this, but I agree with Bea," Dena stood up and said.

I yelled, "You guys don't even know if she's alive or not and all y'all care about is still being in someone's sorority?"

"Do you think Sharon would want us to quit?" Trisha asked.

I almost laughed, "Are you joking? Sharon wanted to quit herself."

"I know everybody thinks differently," Audria said, "and that's okay, but maybe we should put all of our focus on Sharon right now. We can worry about what happens with the line later."

"That's good in theory," Bea said, "But, if Ms. Berry asks us what happened and we don't all share the same response, then those of us who weren't thinking about throwing in the towel will be messed up anyways."

"Ladies! I got here as fast as I could," Cynthia Berry said, rushing toward us.

The five of us looked at each other. We knew we were in trouble.

"I need to know all of the details. I need to know all that is going on with Sharon. I called her mom and of course she is extremely devastated and doesn't understand how this could have happened. Would you guys quit looking at each other and give me some answers," Ms. Berry demanded.

Bea hit me in the knee and I looked up. At first, I was excited about the doctor heading our way—we wouldn't have to answer our advisor. But then I grabbed my chest when I saw he wasn't smiling. It seemed he had bad news.

"I asked you girls to answer me."

"Well, Ms. Berry, the doctor is right here," Bea said.

"Oh, okay," Ms. Berry said, as the doctor approached us.

"You girls are with the young lady?" the doctor asked, before turning to Ms. Berry. "Are you her mom?"

"No, her mom is on her way. I am an advisor to a group on campus that the patient is in."

"Well, okay. She is in serious condition, but I'm glad that these young ladies got her here when they did. She's stable now and I think she is going to be okay."

The five of us jumped for joy and whooped louder than we would at any basketball game. The doctor said she was going to be okay! God is good.

"Do you guys know what caused the reaction?"

"Yes, it was peanut butter, she's allergic to peanuts," I said.

"Knowing that it causes this kind of reaction, I'm a little shocked as to why she would have eaten it. Did she not know that what she was eating had peanuts in it?" he asked.

We all looked at each other. No one wanted to reveal that the food had been forced down her throat. So we looked everywhere but at him.

"Can we see her, Doc?" I asked after the awkward moment passed.

"Not right now, she's got to get some rest," he said.

I asked, "We can wait though and then maybe later we can see her?"

"At least give her another hour to let the medicine work and get some of the swelling in her face and body down."

"Swelling in the face and body? I've got to see this girl," Ms. Berry said.

"Again ma'am, let some time pass for the medicine to do its work. She is going to be okay though. Let me get back to her now," the doctor said before turning away.

"Okay girls, the doctor posed some great questions. It was peanut butter, something she was allergic to. What were you thinking? What were you guys doing? Why did Edythe call me and not you guys? Were you all with her? I know about a Beta sandwich. Did someone force her to eat one?"

Dena looked like she wanted to blab it all out but Trisha was standing right beside her, pulling on her jacket. Audria just looked away, because her face gave it all away.

I already felt like I failed Sharon by convincing her to stay a part of this group when she felt so strongly about wanting to leave. Knowing that now she was okay, it just didn't seem right to keep quiet.

"Oh, let me tell you ladies something right here—I am going to get to the bottom of this. I told you all before this started I was not going to put my organization in jeopardy for any of you guys. I've been a chapter advisor working with these Betas for nine years now. I know every one of them and I know those who will come back to haze. If you guys were intimidated and pressured into doing something, why didn't you come to me?"

That was such a great question. Why didn't we ask Ms. Berry for help? This was all so very hard. But we had felt trapped between what we knew to be right and what we wanted to be known for—not a paper line.

She continued, "I can protect you, but if you won't tell me what happened and I find out on my own that there was madness, rest assured, all of this is gone."

PLEASURE

I took no pleasure in sitting before Sharon's limp body. Though they told me she was going to be fine, it just killed me to see her helpless in the hospital. It had been two days and she had shown signs of improvement, but she was still weak. I just couldn't bring myself to go anywhere. All I had been doing for the past forty-eight hours was talking to God and weeping tears of shame. Lowering my head to weep again, I didn't even see Sharon wake up.

I was startled when she said, "Come on now, Hayden, don't cry. I'm okay."

I sprang to my feet, went over to her bed, and hugged her tight, making sure I didn't touch any of the cords that connected her to the monitors. "You're awake. They said you were going to be okay, but to actually see you awake, oh my gosh!"

"Well, if you knew I was going to be okay, why all the

crying? Yesterday when Bea and Dena visited me they told me you were all upset and that you were taking this personally like this was your fault."

"I do feel like this is my fault, Sharon," I said, as I held her hand.

It was good to see her now with color back in her face. Though her voice was raspy and low, at least she was talking. I was overjoyed that the Lord had answered our prayers and made her better. However, I still felt responsible.

Looking away I said, "You wanted to quit this whole thing. You didn't want to participate anymore and I basically forced you into staying and it ended up being the worst decision I could have ever made."

"Like you knew Keisha was going to flip out, flex her muscles and force me to eat peanut butter. I don't know what kind of people she's around, but I don't lie about stuff I'm allergic to. She was so careless in giving it to me anyway. Before any of us could react it was in my mouth, and as you now see just a pinch of that stuff is lethal for me."

"Oh Sharon, we all were so furious with her," I said, extremely frustrated as I reflected back.

"I remember a little bit of it. I was so out of it. It was hard because I couldn't breathe and I felt stupid for not leaving at the first sight of the peanut butter. But I remember she didn't even want you guys to call the ambulance. She is just crazy."

"Yeah," I responded. "She only cares about herself."

"Have you talked to the Betas? Are you still doing any more of that underground stuff?"

"No," I told her, truly knowing in my heart I would never go back to any of that underground craziness.

"Bea and Dena were in here yesterday, both pleading their cases and trying to convince me not to rat out the Betas."

"I can't believe they'd bug you with that," I said.

She tried to sit up. Her stiff body could not take it. The discomfort on her face was real.

"Don't move, relax," I said.

"No, no. I'm torn, Hayden, and I respect you so much. For goodness sake, you're sitting in my room crying, hoping that I am okay. It is pretty clear you are an awesome leader. You care about more than just yourself. I want to be that type of person. I know I am a little moody more times than not, but I have had a lot of time to think while I've been in this hospital bed. When you think your life is about to end, and God gives you another chance, then you got to do something with it. So can you please tell me what I should do?"

This was amazing to me. She admired me when I felt so unworthy of her respect. I already felt like I led her wrong once. There was no way I was going to give her bad advice again.

"I actually need you to tell me what you want me to do, Sharon. I've been dodging Cynthia Berry for a couple of days, but before I came into your room, she called me to tell me she was on her way up here with the Regional Coordinator. I think they know foul play was involved."

"So you're saying if I tell them the truth, you don't care if the whole line gets dropped? Hayden, I know how much you want to be a Beta."

I bent down toward her so she could clearly see my eyes and said, "Now might not be the right time for me to be a Beta. I can only truly live with myself and be at peace if I tell the truth about what happened to you."

A sincere smile came upon her frail face. Standing up for the only thing that was right made me feel better than I had in a while. Pleasing God meant more to me than getting any Greek letters. Sharon reached out her arms and I pulled her into a hug.

When we came out of our embrace, there was a knock at the door. I turned around and in walked Sharon's mother; our advisor, Cynthia Berry; Deborah Nixon, the Regional Coordinator; and both the east and west Arkansas State Directors. A lump formed in my throat, but I knew I had to get it out. I had to stand true to my word and follow through with what I just told Sharon. As the line president, I needed to spill the beans. I owed everyone the benefit of telling the truth.

Deborah Nixon came over to Sharon and said, "Boy, am I excited to see you well. We don't want to stay here long. I want to be straight with you. We are here to get to the bottom of exactly what happened."

Sharon's mom cut in and said, "Yeah, I told them I was extremely upset and if I need to sue the national organization, I will do it because this absolutely makes no sense."

Ms. Nixon said, "Your mother is right. This is ridiculous. If you were put here under duress we need you and your line sisters to tell us exactly what happened."

When Trisha and Bea walked in, I knew they looked disappointed in me. They wanted the line be on, but they knew I wasn't going to stand for any more lies.

"So is anybody going to say anything?" Ms. Berry said.

I stepped toward her and said, "Ma'am, I'm Hayden Grant, and on behalf of the line, I'd like to give a full statement of what happened. See, we were . . ."

"No, no, I think I need to talk since it happened to me," Sharon said, catching me off guard.

Because I knew her, I could tell she was faking up a cry. What was she doing? Why didn't she let me have her back?

"Please don't get emotional," Ms. Nixon said to her.

"No, you just don't understand. We worked so hard and it wasn't our fault. I don't want us to lose everything. It just wouldn't be fair."

"That's what I was trying to tell them, baby," her momma said. "It's going to be okay. Ms. Nixon, please tell them what you told me."

"Well, if it comes out that you guys were bullied and under duress, even though you signed a statement saying you wouldn't participate in hazing, your line will go forward."

I looked over at Trisha and Bea and their faces completely changed. Big smiles were etched on their faces. Between Trisha, Dena, Audria, Sharon, Bea and myself they got more information than they bargained for.

To our surprise, later that same night, with the regional and state officials in town, our line was inducted. The alumnae sorors rushed to plan something to get us past all the intense tension. Plus, the Alpha chapter undergrads were no longer allowed to have anything to do with us.

Bea said, "I can't believe we're crossing over. Hayden and Trisha, I love you both."

"I know I'm tough, and I pushed us hard to endure the crap. Forgive me, y'all," Trisha said.

We were so excited that we couldn't stand it. We'd been on such a head trip. The low of Sharon's incident was devastating, but now I was on such a high, I believe I was touching the sky. God had granted my desire to be a part of Beta Gamma Pi. Deep in my heart I wanted to honor His blessing.

I walked through the icy coals to get to the other side of Beta Gamma Pi and reach sisterhood. I gave my pledge to serve the organization all of my life and to sustain the values, beliefs, and goals of Beta Gamma Pi. Because my mom was just thirty minutes across town, Ms. Berry got in touch with her. It warmed my heart to have her pin me.

"You guys went through way more than any line should," she whispered in my ear, her eyes heavy with regret.

"I just felt I had to make sure they knew Grant women were legitimate Betas," I said, alluding to the fact that the big sisters had gaven her pledge process no respect.

She held me tight and said, "Oh Hayden, baby, you didn't have to go through any of this for me. You know by now I don't care what people say. Besides, if I misled you to feel that I wasn't satisfied with how I crossed then I was wrong. I wanted to pledge back in college, but because of all the love and knowledge I received when I was on the graduate line, I'd never trade if I could."

Wiping the tears from my eyes, I said, "I believe that now, Mom."

"I'm sad you didn't call me, Hayden. I could've stopped some of that foolishness."

"Well Mom, you told me not to participate in any of that stuff in the first place. How could I call you when I violated the rules?"

"We all make stupid decisions. It just makes sense to learn from them. A girl on your line almost lost her life, sweetheart. Where in the world is the sisterhood in that?"

It was weird crossing without Penelope, Edythe, and even crazy Keisha being there. Though I didn't know what was going to happen to them, I knew not being there to take their own line over would be a big blow to some of them.

With the regional officers there, we got permission to participate in the campus-wide probate show. We and the Pi's were the last lines to cross. It's standard at our school that the probate show is the night of the last line crossing over. It was hard to plan because no one knew when that would be. Our performance was abbreviated because we were missing Sharon, who was still in the hospital. We had just started learning the exhibition dances usually performed, but because of everything that happened we'd only learned two steps. We were so thrilled to be Betas, that on the two numbers we did do, we showed out and had everybody in the audience on their feet giving us props.

After all of the sororities probated, the men went. My heart skipped a beat when I saw Creed do a lead-off step, but after he was done, several women rushed up to him.

My heart dropped. With all of the drama going on, I hadn't done my part in keeping in touch. So I couldn't blame him for entertaining others. Guess we were over before we began.

"Hayden, wait! Where you going, baby?" I heard him say from over my shoulder, as I walked in the opposite direction.

I stopped and slowly turned. I didn't know how to respond. I wanted him but I'd dropped the ball.

"I miss you," he said to me, as he took my breath away. "What, you don't feel the same no more?"

"No, it's not like that at all," I said, inwardly smiling. "You were just occupied and I didn't want to interrupt you. After all, I hadn't been in touch because we'd both been on line. It would have been nice to connect with you, but you were in my thoughts. I couldn't even call you."

"What are you talking about? I just assumed we both understood," Creed said, seemingly cool that we'd both been out of touch.

"Well, I thought that had to be the case," I said to him, "Since you were with other girls."

"Whatever," Creed said sternly. "My whole line wants to talk to you, but that's not gonna stop me from being with you. You shoulda sashayed your cute behind over to me and all the honeys and let them know I was taken, but because you didn't, no need to get wrong. I ain't letting you go nowhere. I want a kiss."

Not caring who was looking at me, I was happy to fall into his arms and comply with his request. A man's lips never felt so inviting, so warm, so soothing, so surreal, and so relaxing. Creed still cared about me and that really mattered to me.

"Excuse me, excuse me," Bea said, cutting in between the two of us. "You forgot your momma was out here somewhere."

"Your mom's here?" Creed asked, eyeing me down.

I blushed and said, "Yeah, I would like to introduce you if that's alright?"

"First you need to introduce yourself to her uncle. Hayden, I didn't know you were talking to this one. Creed is now my frat brother."

Uncle Wade put his arm around Creed. I thought he was going to say something nice. When he tightened his grip on my guy, however, I cringed. "I didn't like all that lip action I just witnessed, especially out in public. Respect my niece. You understand?"

"Yes sir, will . . . will do, sir," Creed said, tripping over his words.

"Hayden, take him over there to meet my sister. But Creed, you go partying with your frat brothers after this. Leave her alone, you two don't need to be celebrating together. You understand?" my uncle said.

"Yes sir," Creed responded quickly.

"Sorry about that," Creed caringly whispered in my ear. "I didn't know he was your uncle."

"Yep, we try and keep it under wraps, so I can just go to school without special treatment. That's why I mentioned, the day I saw your face all bruised up, that I'd tell the President. He's cool. I forgot the world was around us looking. I missed you so much, I just got caught up in the moment," I told him in a seductive tone.

Creed nodded. "How about I meet your mom and we play it off like we're going in different directions, and in an hour we'll hook up at my place. Is that aight?"

"So you mean you got your place back?" I joked, remembering that the guys who pledged him were staked out at his place.

"Not yet, but I'm kicking everybody out of it tonight. It might not be the cleanest, but it'll be something special for me and you."

It was hard to contain my excitement. After I introduced Creed to my mom, he smiled and went over to his boys. She tugged on my shirt and said, "Okay sweetie, I can see from the way the young man was looking at you that this is serious. What's going on with the two of y'all?"

"Nothing Mom, I mean he's my boyfriend, but we're taking it slow."

"Sweetheart, you just crossed and you got so much going on right now, leave the young man alone."

"Why do you say that? You didn't like him, Mom? He didn't seem nice?"

"Yeah, he seems great. I just don't want you to get yourself in more trouble than you need to. Remember even when I am not watching, God is."

"Mom, did you have to throw that on me?"

"Yeah, I needed to put the fear of God in your heart. Don't do what you are not supposed to do with a more experienced boy."

I gave her a hug and she left with the rest of the moms who came to watch the ceremony.

An hour could not have passed fast enough for me. I was at Creed's apartment waiting for him, but after an hour and a half, I felt like he let the excitement of partying with his frat brothers get in between us having our special time. Just as I was about to dip his car pulled in. He rushed up to my window.

"I'm sorry, baby," he said. "I got caught up with the fellas, but I'll make it up to you, I promise."

When we got inside, the place was a mess. I could tell that his line had been using his place as headquarters.

"Nobody used my guest bedroom though," he said as he led me in there and put some Luther Vandross on the CD player. "I missed you, you know that. It was so hard on line some days, but when I thought about you I was able to get through them, Hayden. I want to be with you. I want to make you feel good."

Reflecting back, things were starting to work out. Sharon was okay and I was a Beta. I needed to relax. As my boyfriend's hands slid down my pants and his lips found mine, I had to admit, I'd never felt such pleasure.

10

BROKEN

Okay, Lord, his hands are all over my breasts and I can't stop thinking about You not being pleased with what's going on here. I've been a virgin for nineteen years. Is that not enough? Why can't I enjoy this moment? I finally got something I really wanted and now I have this guy too. Darn, I want him so much, but is this right?

"Okay, so what's up? You're not into this," Creed said, breaking my prayer. "I'm touching you. I'm feeling you. I'm trying to kiss you and I ain't getting no love back. C'mon now. This don't feel good? You're breaking my heart."

"It's not that it doesn't feel good," I said as I took the cover off the bed and used it to cover my bare body.

"You're not shy all of a sudden, are you, baby?"

"Well, it has just been a second, and you haven't seen me that much. I am a little shy. Is that okay?" I said, getting a little annoyed that he was upset with me.

Besides, this was my body. This was my right. If I wasn't ready then he needed to accept that and move on. I wasn't some little girl that would be shattered and broken if he decided not to fool with me again.

"So if I don't give it up, we're through?" I said. I needed to cut straight to the chase.

"Why you sayin' all that? And why are you acting so mean?" he questioned.

"This is all new for me and I don't want to go so fast. I know you got your letters now and there are so many girls that will easily give it up."

"Let's just set the record straight. I could have women without these letters. Nowadays all you gotta do is tell them what they want to hear and they give up the booty."

"Okay then. So maybe I'm not the girl for you. I'm not gonna be so quick to give it up. I've heard the sweet words before. I've got it going on too, Creed. And if I'm not worth waiting for, in your mind, then I'm glad I didn't give it up to you now."

"But Hayden, you're putting words in my mouth. I didn't say that if we didn't have sex I was out of here. You know I mean every word I say to you. No bull here. I really care for you. And I mean it when I say you helped me get through a tough pledge period. I would be lying if I said I wasn't thinking about taking our relationship to the next level. Being with you, celebrating both of our joys, it gets me going. But if you're not ready, I respect that. But can a brother get a little affection? Can I talk you through some of this? What's got you so scared?"

I didn't know how he was going to take my Christian values, but I guess it was important we talk about that because I just didn't want a relationship built on the pleasures of the flesh. I needed a relationship built on the spirit, where God was at the center of our relationship. For us to withstand the temptation our bodies were feeling we needed divine intervention.

I didn't know I could feel such pleasure and I truly didn't want that feeling to end. But for God it had to. Imagining my dad watching me from over in Iraq was one thing, but to envision the Heavenly Father upset in Heaven, was even more unsettling. I didn't want to block His blessing for the rest of my life. No telling what one bad action would do to the plans He had for me.

Putting on my shirt, I sat on the edge of the bed and said, "You know, I don't know how you're going to take this, but I just didn't want to displease the Lord. You gonna go run away now or what? Oh, I forgot this is your place, I'm the one that needs to leave," I said, getting up from the bed.

He stood up too and hugged me. "You don't need to go nowhere. I believe in God, Jesus, all that. I don't want Him mad at me either, messing with one of the last pure, special creatures He has on this earth. I'ma prove to you that I'm worthy. I've been out there a little too much. I gotta admit, I wasn't trying to save myself for nobody. But I have had empty nights with women. I feel there's a connection with you. I don't wanna ruin what I think is developing here. Let's just continue to work with each other until we figure all this out. Is that cool?"

"Yeah," I said, as he pulled me back to the bed.

I felt whole. My first night as a Beta and I was sleeping in my man's arms. He understood me and cared. *Thank you, Jesus.*

I woke up the next morning to the constant ringing of my cell phone. Creed and I tried to ignore it the first couple of times, but whoever needed me wouldn't stop calling.

"You better answer it. Obviously somebody's really trying to get you," he said, stroking my neck.

Being a little overly conscious of my morning breath, I turned away from him and said, "Probably my roommate Chandra wanting to make sure I'm okay."

"Well answer it," he said. "Let her know you're cool."

"Hello?" I said without even looking at the caller ID. "I'm okay, girl. I'll be home in a bit."

"Who do you think this is?" Bea asked.

"Bea?" I said, catching her voice.

"Yeah, it's me."

"Oh, never mind. What's going on?" I said, as I pulled the covers and sat up.

"Why won't you answer your phone?" she asked me.

"Girl, what's up?"

"You're with that Pi dude, aren't you? A girl gets some letters and she just loses her mind."

"Miss Smarty, he was my man before we crossed," I said, a little salty.

"And you kept that from all of us?"

"Bea, what did you call me for?"

"Oh, yeah, yeah, yeah," she said. "Penelope needs her phone back. I just needed to know if you wanted me to go with you to take it back to her since she needs it really bad."

"Oh snap, I've had it for a couple of days," I said.

"Yeah, I guess so."

"Does she know that we crossed?" I asked Bea.

"She didn't say anything to me, but she sounded pretty upset. So I assume she does. Plus, we were on the yard. I'm up for going with you if you need me to. She said she's at her apartment and you know where that is."

"I'm straight."

As soon as I hung up the phone, Creed asked, "Is everything alright?"

"Yeah, just line drama."

"You wanna talk to me?"

"Nah, it's sorority stuff. I'm cool. You understand, right?" I said, giving him a kiss on his luscious lips.

"Alright, go take care of that. Call me though."

"I will, and thanks for being more than a gentleman."

"I'm your guy. You wouldn't hook up with just anybody, would you?" he said, making me smile.

Fifteen minutes later, I was standing in front of Penelope's door. She must have been looking out for me, because the front door swung open. Her apartment was incredible. On the sly, I peered around her to notice a large living room with rosy red curtains, a fluffy matching rug in the center of the room, and classy black-and-white posters of Billie Holiday and Langston Hughes that adorned the walls. Penelope's place was hot.

"Can I have my phone?" she said, her eyes red and swollen.

She looked like she hadn't slept in days. I had made sure that I took off all the Beta Gamma Pi paraphernalia I was wearing for the probate show the day before. No need to get into any questions or flaunt anything in her face. Though I didn't know what happened to her, Edythe or Keisha, I knew it wasn't going to be pretty.

"Are you going to be okay?" I said, handing her the phone.

She snatched it from my grasp and said, "Please don't act like you care about me. You're a Beta now. You don't need me for anything except respect. And with how you guys messed us all up, you probably won't be earning any of that any time soon."

In my mind, I had thought that they would probably have to pay a fine, and maybe Keisha would be the only one suspended. I knew we were going to have to get along with them though. I didn't want such hostility between us.

Trying, I said, "We're sisters now. We'll all find a way to get past this."

"Are you kidding? All of us are being suspended for five years. We can't go to sorority meetings, wear any paraphernalia, participate in any activities that you guys host or any other Beta chapter for that matter. If that's not enough, our names are listed on the national website as outcasts. Also, we'll each have to pay a twenty-five hundred dollar fine before we can even think about coming back into the fold. National does not play when it comes to hazing."

I just stood there with my mouth open. I really didn't understand what this meant so I said, "You're Vice President. What about Edythe?"

Turning away, she said, "All of us are gone. There may even be repercussions from the school because of our illegal actions. You guys are on your own now. You ratted us out. It seems like you wanted this."

I looked her right in the eye so she could tell I did care. "No we didn't. We wanted Keisha to get the punishment that she was due, but you tried to defend us. It just got out of hand. That wasn't the first time y'all's actions left someone seriously hurt. We didn't even tell Nationals all of that."

"You're right. I know I failed you guys and as hard as I tried to protect you, I was just as guilty as Keisha."

"That's not what I'm saying," I said, huffing.

"You don't have to say it. That's how I feel and that's how the regional officers saw it. Go on. Get away from my door and be a better Beta than I was."

Later that night there was a meeting called by the Regional Coordinator and our advisor. We were meeting on campus in our sorority office. This was the first time we were privy to its space. The room had Beta Gamma Pi pictures and plaques all over the walls. This was Alpha chapter, and the rich history that surrounded us was moving. The room's centerpiece was a large, elegant frame of our sorority's founders—similar to the one I remembered from our initiation ceremony. Beneath the frame was a small gold plaque that outlined the details of the photo and reminded us all of the reasons we chose to become Betas:

A SISTERHOOD COMMITTED TO MAKING THE WORLD
GREATER. OUR ELITE FOUNDERS. THESE FIVE EXTRA-
ORDINARY WOMEN OF CHARACTER AND VIRTUE
FOUNDED BETA GAMMA PI ON THE CAMPUS OF
WESTERN SMITH COLLEGE. GREAT SERVICE. GREAT
LEADERSHIP. GREAT PROGRESS. SINCE 1919.

During the meeting, our Regional Coordinator and
chapter advisor confirmed what Penelope had told me
earlier. All of the girls that were in the chapter were suspended. Now we had to hold elections. Unanimously, I
was voted Chapter President. Clearly, it was an office I
wasn't ready for. I had just joined the sorority. I didn't
know much at all. All I wanted was justice, but for Penelope and Edythe, the punishment they had gotten, though
truthfully more than fair, was heart wrenching.

I hadn't been the most effective leader, though I had
only been in office a week. I hadn't called any meetings. It
was December and it was time for semester finals, so we
hadn't planned any functions. I just felt everybody needed
to go their own way and study for exams. But then I got a
call from Ms. Berry. It wasn't like she was the advisor
from hell, but she did have high expectations of what the
sisterhood and our chapter were supposed to do.

"Hayden, you guys are Alpha chapter. You're not just
there to parade around campus wearing lavender and
turquoise letters and be at everybody's party. Where's the
public service? There's always an annual end-of-the-year
project that you guys do to help the community. You all
know this because you've seen the chapter history. I

know it's difficult for you to come in and make big decisions, but we need true leadership."

She didn't know at all how difficult this was for me. We had to see the suspended Betas around campus whispering to other people that we were the ones that got them kicked off. And then of course girls from my line let it leak that the Betas almost killed Sharon so they should be happy that they just got kicked off, instead of being in jail. And for Keisha that was still a real possibility because Sharon's mom was extremely angry. However, being the chapter president of a divided group was just as tough mentally as all the physical drama I had to deal with while I was on line.

Ms. Berry looked at her calendar, where she kept a listing of all of the chapter events, and saw we had a highway cleanup project scheduled. I called all of my ice chips, the girls who'd been through the ice with me, and gave them the time and the place and info of what we needed to do. But when I showed up at the designated spot with a trash bag, I was completely disappointed that none of them came. I ended up calling Chandra and Creed to come by and help.

When Creed and Chandra got there, Creed jokingly said, "So your girls just ditched you?"

"This isn't funny," I said to him.

"Well they're out partying all over campus. Did you really think they were going to do any public service in the first place?" Chandra said to me.

"They're grown women. There's nothing I can do," I said to the both of them.

Creed put down his trash bag. "That's not true. You're

the Chapter President. They voted you to keep them straight. Get on their butts if you need to."

Chandra said, "If nothing else, at least remind them of why y'all supposedly signed up to be in a sorority in the first place. Because I got a couple of them in my class and they keep coming in late and are obviously hung over. I'll be surprised if most of them even pass their finals."

"But I'm leaving to go home for Christmas break tomorrow. I can't get us all together in time."

"Well obviously you can't get them together if they think it's to do some work," Creed said.

"What, you want me to lie to them?"

"Nah, but you need to make it sound urgent. You know how to get them. Please, do your thing. Work what you got," he said, looking at me. "All of my brothers are talking about them. I'm just saying you don't want your girls to have a bad reputation."

Five hours later we were in our sorority room on campus. My urgent call for a meeting worked. Everyone including Sharon was there.

"What's going on, girl? What's so important?" Trisha asked.

"Yeah, there's a fraternity party tonight and we need to be up in the place," Audria said, completely shocking me. She had been the good girl on the line. What had happened to her? If she had turned crazy, there was no hope for any of us. Was I so into my own world that I never noticed how Audria, a preacher girl, dismissed her religion so quickly? I had to do something. I had to let them know their actions weren't faring well for BGP.

"Guys, there's been a lot of folks coming to me and telling me that my line sisters are all wild. And I know we're supposed to have fun and enjoy this newfound world of Greekdom we're in, but we're not supposed to go crazy. I love each of you guys, I do. But we vowed to uphold the values and ideals of this sorority. We're here to help the community. Today we were supposed to pick up trash and y'all were picking up men. I believe our founders would turn over in their graves if they could see how you guys were acting. These letters are not about us. They are about bettering the world. You guys need to check yourselves, and I'm doing the same thing, because obviously as a leader I'm failing if you think all we're here for is to party. In order for us to do Alpha chapter proud, we gotta get our priorities straight. We gotta fix this because right now this Beta Gamma Pi chapter is broken."

GUILTY

Trisha stood up and said to everyone, "Self-centered, Greek-letter wearing heffas is what we have been. Hayden, you're right."

After I had given my big spiel about how disappointed I was in all of them for not showing up for the public service project, I felt bad that I had been so harsh. Everyone deserved to have a little fun. But hearing Trisha accept everything I had to say with the right spirit really made me feel good. However, no one else was saying anything. Then my cell phone rang. I had forgotten to turn it off before the meeting had begun. I quickly answered it. "Yeah, what's up?"

"Hey, it's me, Creed. I'm just touching base with you. I know you were meeting up with your girls. Is everything straight?"

"You're interrupting. I'm in the middle of that meeting right now!"

"I'm sorry, don't bite my head off. I was just checking," he replied.

"I'm sorry. I have to call you back. I should have turned off my phone."

"Alright, call me back . . ."

I hung up before he could even finish. I was bummed with how I was treating my line sisters and ashamed at how I was treating my man. All this pressure to sit here and do the right thing was obviously weighing me down. Christmas break couldn't come soon enough.

Audria came over to me and placed her hand on my shoulder and said, "And that's why we wanted you to lead us, so you could keep us on track, and reel us in like wild fish trying to get away from the bait. Thanks for personally calling me out. I'm going to straighten up, and put God first."

"Yeah, I'm going to straighten up too," Dena said.

"And I told them we should be picking up trash, but they blew me off," Sharon blurted out.

We all laughed and a couple of people balled up paper and threw it at her. Obviously, she was having fun like everyone else. I was proud of the support. Maybe we could turn it all around.

So I said, "Alright, we can't go back. We've had a little fun and now it's time to get a little perspective and really do this thing like we said we would when we signed up to be members of Beta Gamma Pi."

Trisha, our elected treasurer, raised her hand and said, "Well, I think we should have a Beta Gamma Pi end-of-the-school-year bash, like they did last year. We're low on funds and we need to put some money in the pot."

"Yeah, let's do it," Bea agreed.

I was starting to think about what she was saying and I wasn't opposed to it. But I just told them that we had been doing too much of that. I wasn't sure a party was the right move. Plus, with all our pledging funds it didn't make sense for the account to be low.

"I don't understand how the account can be low." I questioned Trisha.

"I don't know, maybe all of the checks haven't cleared from the ones that we submitted to pledge," Trisha replied.

"But we didn't submit checks," Dena said.

"Yeah," I reminded Trisha, "we used money orders. The account shouldn't be low. Let me see the bank statement."

"Uhh, I don't . . . I don't—" Trisha couldn't give me a straight answer. "You know what, I don't have it on me. I didn't know we were going to go through all of this business."

I said, "That's cool! I just don't think a party is the way we need to go about raising money."

Trisha appealed to my heart and said, "Well, we need to come back next semester with some funds so that we can really make an impact on the community. I'm not one for parties, but we need a quick fix. Let's take a vote."

I was quickly outvoted. That night, at five dollars a head, we filled the clubhouse at Trisha's apartment complex. It got a little uncomfortable when five of the suspended Betas: Penelope, Edythe, Keisha and two other sorors, came to the door. Protocol didn't allow us to charge them, suspended or not. It was the first time any of us had been in contact with Keisha, and we all froze when we saw her.

"Y'all go on in," Trisha said.

Penelope grabbed my arm and led me over to a corner. "What's going on with all of these parties y'all are attending and now hosting? The event we do at the end of the semester is supposed to be public service based."

Keeping it real, I said, "We were just trying to get some more money in the account."

"There was forty-five hundred dollars in the account when we turned everything over to the Regional Coordinator. How much money do y'all need?" she said, shocking me.

"This party is weak anyway," Keisha came over and said—and just as quickly as she and her crew came in they were gone.

Trisha smiled at me and shrugged her shoulders, not having heard what Penelope had said about the account. I knew I couldn't believe everything I was told, but as much as I loved my girl Trisha, something wasn't right.

"Mom, I'm home," I said as I arrived home for the Christmas break.

I didn't realize how much I had missed being home. The smell of the apple cider, seeing the pretty Christmas tree in the living room and the sound of the Nat King Cole Christmas CD my mom played every year, reminded me I was glad I was home. I couldn't wait to be in her arms, but she was nowhere to be found.

At that point, I couldn't wait to see my sister Hailey either. She usually got on my nerves when I was home. However, being away from the brat made me miss her tail. She wasn't around either. Where was everyone? I had seen my mom's car in the driveway, so surely they were home.

"Mom, it's me, come out. I'm home," I uttered, a little disappointed.

"Yeah, but what you didn't know is that I was coming home," my father called from behind me.

As much as I had missed my mom and my sister, I hadn't seen my dad in two and a half years. Hearing his voice and being in his presence was the best Christmas gift ever. I turned around and almost took his neck off from choking him so tight.

"Aww princess. You don't miss your old man that much. You've been off to college and I can't even get a letter from you. I even tried the texting thing a month back and I got no response. Left you messages on your cell phone, and that didn't even make you get back to me. Your mom says this sorority stuff has your mind completely off track so I had to come home and make sure I still had a daughter at Western Smith College."

"Oh Daddy, I'm sorry," I said, ashamed 'cause I knew he was right.

I had stopped writing. I hadn't even really been there for my younger sister, either. With all the drama at school, I hadn't stopped to think that I still had a family that needed me. Beta Gamma Pi couldn't take up all of my energy.

"Your mom is in my rental. She and your sister are picking up some groceries. They wanted to make everything perfect for you. I think you are an hour or two earlier than she expected. You know she's planning this big dinner. With us both back home, she is going all out."

And then I just cried. I had totally gotten off track. But now I was so happy just to be with my dad.

"I'm sorry, Daddy. I know I have been a horrible daughter. You've been over there fighting and you don't even know what I'm doing. I've thought about you all of the time and I am going to do better, I promise."

"Well, don't worry about that. While I'm back I'll be able to check it out for myself."

The night was so special. We played games and had the best home cooked meal. Even Hailey, my usually bratty sister, was on her best behavior. Having a home away from home with my roommates was great, but it was nothing like actually being with your family.

The next afternoon, my dad took me shopping to catch up. My mom was helping my sister get ready for her piano recital that we'd all be attending shortly. It had been ages since my father and I hung out. He kept looking over at me. Yep, his baby had grown up. He looked like he wanted to discuss something deep. I wished he'd just come out with it, so I could get him to go deep in his pockets and hook me up with some new outfits.

Breaking the ice, I said, "Daddy, are you back for good?"

"Sure am, baby girl."

"Does Mom know?"

"No, not yet. That's my Christmas present to her. She thinks I'm here just for a week. I know it's been hard for you, baby, not having your old man around, but your mom has been keeping me posted."

Now I knew he was about to get to talking. *What has Mom been telling him?* I wondered. Whatever it was, I knew I could always talk to my dad. When I got my first kiss after junior prom in high school, he was the first person I told and he actually didn't trip.

He touched my face and continued, "She told me that

I need to get back here because you have your eyes on some young man. I don't believe you've been sleeping over at any guy's house. But I know you may be tempted. It ain't been that long since I was in college, and I remember how it was—there are certainly some things I did that I am not proud of. But dating is different for men, our reputation can bounce back. I certainly remember telling you before I left here, men don't like buying the cow when they can get the milk for free."

I said, "Exactly."

"So, what's up? You're not doing anything with that boy I wouldn't approve of?"

"Dad."

"See, you look guilty."

"No, Dad. I'm serious. I've been good."

"Well, where is the young man? Am I going to meet him any time soon?"

"I think he's probably mad at me."

"Why?"

"Same reason you are."

"You haven't been calling your guy either? What's going on with this sorority stuff? I never pledged, but I know it's taken a lot out of your mom. I just don't get it. What do you all do that makes you forget the rest of the world?"

I just looked at him. There was no excuse for not communicating with the people who were important to you. It was what it was though. During the next hour, I filled my dad in on what happened during the semester and gave him some of the highlights of my pledge experience.

"You've got to do better, Hayden. You've got to work

with what you've got. It's okay to be the leader of any organization, but you have to know how to spread yourself
around and balance everything you have going on in
your life. Being an officer in the Navy, I cannot stay focused on just one aspect of my job. I have to multitask."

"Don't you feel overwhelmed? A lot of my days, Dad,
I do. But I love my sorority. There's just something about
it. It's brought out a side of me that I didn't know existed.
I care so much for these girls, so much that I want them
to honor their commitments to the sorority."

"Great, you are concerned with causes bigger than
yourselves, but you can't lose your family and your friends
while you're working on new relationships, you know?
You're so bright and intelligent. I know you're going to
figure all of this out."

"I just feel bad."

"No need to feel bad. Fix it."

"Yes sir," I said, smiling and happy to be in my daddy's
arms again.

Oh, what a blessing to have a dad that cares so much.
I so needed his reality check. BGP was important to me,
it wasn't all I had. I had to find a balance.

"I'm so sorry we didn't get together over the holidays," I said to Creed over the phone.

"I'm just saying, Hayden, I know you have other stuff,
but if you want a relationship, it takes both of us. Over
the Christmas holidays, I don't hear from my girl at all,
and now we're back at school and you're trying to call
me. I don't know."

"My dad was in town and he's been gone for two and a half years, so I was spending all of my time with him. I didn't know he was coming. I'm sorry."

"I would have liked to meet your pops. What, you didn't want to bring me around him or even return my calls?"

I really had no answer for Creed. I did feel bad, horrible really. But if I had to do it all over again, I wasn't sure that I would have chosen spending time with him over my family. It had been so long since the four of us could just be that—a family. It was special, but I couldn't even explain it before my other line started ringing. From the caller ID I could see it was Dena.

"It's one of . . ." I said, but Creed cut me off.

"Your line sisters."

"Yeah, being chapter president is crazy."

"Take care of it." Then he hung up.

"Hey girl!" I said, trying not to put my frustrations on Dena.

"Oh my gosh, Hayden, this is horrible."

"What?"

"Our checking account is wrong."

"I don't know what you mean, start over."

"Well, after the dance, I counted the money with Trisha and I know we counted five hundred and eighty dollars, but the deposit was only for two hundred and eighty. I wasn't three hundred dollars off. I did have a wine cooler or two, but I wasn't that off," Dena said in a panicked tone.

"Well, did you ask Trisha about the discrepancy?" I asked, trying to give Trisha the benefit of the doubt.

"Yeah, and she says that I signed for two hundred and

eighty. My signature is on the deposit slip, but I know it's more than that."

"Well," I said, scratching my head, "I didn't even count the money, and I know it was more than three hundred. That doesn't even sound right."

"She said we bought drinks and stuff, and that we had to pay for the clubhouse and that took up money, but there's not even a record of us taking in five hundred and eighty and then spending it out somewhere. It's just not right, Hayden."

"Alright, thanks for calling me. Have you talked to anyone else?" I asked her, trying to really get an understanding of the situation I was dealing with here.

Already suspecting that Trisha was dipping into our account, I knew this was serious. The old heads had already let me know we had tons of money in our account. Then we have a party and we still come up with practically no money.

"No, no," Dena said, "I just saw this. She wanted to go over the books before our chapter meeting."

"Okay girl, I'll see you at the meeting."

Immediately, I got into my car and went over to see Bea. She was elected first Vice President. I knew she cared about Trisha like I did. The three of us went way back to the underground line. Bea could help me figure all this out.

"What am I supposed to do? Penelope told me there was forty-five hundred dollars in the account. Dena says that they counted almost double what was actually put into the bank account from the party. I don't know what Trisha is thinking. You of all people understand what we have gone through with the underground line being dropped and being the only ones who went through all of that crap. For her to take us through more is ridiculous. Come on, Trisha is our girl. She had my back on the line. I can't believe she is taking money. I don't want to have a meeting and reveal this with everybody there. What should I do?"

"I'm supposed to be the one that's telling you to keep it under wraps, she's our girl, let's clean it up and fix it. And if I were president that is probably what I would do, Hayden. But I'm not president. I don't have the backbone that you do to stand up against wrongdoing. Everybody in our chapter has a right to talk to her about this. She needs to be caught off guard so she can't fix her story. If there is nothing to tell, we'll just call the whole ordeal a mix-up. She loves you, Hayden. She'll understand."

"Alright, will you pick Trisha up and I'll text everyone else to get down here and meet in our sorority room on campus."

An hour and a half later, I had all of them in front of me. My heart felt sick believing all this could be true about my girl. I so hoped it would come out that this was a misunderstanding.

"I've got studying to do," Trisha said, standing up. "What's this all about?"

Bea said, "Girl, we just got back on campus and exams are over. Come on, you've got the lowest GPA out of all of us."

"Alright, well let me cut to the chase," I said, not in the mood for her to yank my chain and play me anymore. "Trisha, we need to see the bank account books."

"Umm, Dena and I are working on that and going over it. Let us get it exactly straight before we show you. Right, Dena?"

"No," Dena said, "we went through everything. And there's some stuff not adding up for me."

Trisha laughed. "Oh Dena, don't exaggerate. I can show you guys that stuff tomorrow. This isn't urgent."

"Yeah, it is urgent, Trisha," I said boldly to the girl we all trusted with our money. "Penelope told me there was forty-five hundred dollars in our account when they turned everything over to the Regional Coordinator and the advisor. But you said there was no money in the account."

"Well, how much did we bring in from the party?" Sharon said. "It had to be like six hundred dollars, because when I counted with y'all it was like four something . . ."

"See, I knew it," Dena jumped up and said. "You took some money, Trisha."

Dena went over to Trisha's face and got ugly. Then the two started arguing. Bea went over and pulled the two of them apart. All the sorors were hot at Trisha.

"Okay, y'all, okay," Trisha finally admitted with a scratch over her eye. "I've been taking some money. Sorry."

"How could you do that to us?" Audria asked.

"Because I'm going to get kicked out of school. I don't have the tuition money. I'm applying for a few grants and they look promising. I figured once I got the money I was going to put it back before anyone would notice. I betrayed everyone's trust. I'm sorry, I just felt I had no choice. I couldn't throw my education out the window. As chapter treasurer, I know I have abused my powers. I'm guilty."

PROBLEM

I went over to Trisha. I really appreciated the fact that she came clean to all of us. We needed to be told what was going on. Though her confession was a good start there was a lot of animosity. None of us in the chapter had money coming out of the butt, we all had monetary issues.

"Trisha, you're not the only one with problems, girl," Bea yelled out in disgust.

"Yeah, I don't even know how I'm going to pay my rent," Dena replied. "I can't believe that you put the wrong amount of money in the bank and forged my name on a deposit slip. Trisha, that messes up my name."

Audria said, "We need the money back now, Trisha."

"I don't have it, y'all, that's what I'm sayin'," Trisha responded in tears.

"Well, we need to call the Regional Coordinator about this then," Sharon said.

"No guys, no, you can't call and tell on me. I will pay the money back. I promise."

Most girls looked away. They couldn't stand to face her. She went over to Bea, desperately seeking sympathy.

With distraught red eyes, Bea looked at Trisha and said, "You've become my girl. I've always had you and Hayden's back on line and in my heart. The three of us have started to rap about everything. Maybe if you would've just come to us, Trisha, told us what was going on, we could have figured out a way to help you. But to just go into the account and withdraw the money, forging people's signatures on stuff for your own personal gain, is just something I can't accept."

Bea sat down in a chair and bowed her head. I knew this was hard for her. She was right, Trisha was our girl. This was tough.

Bea stood and continued, "We got to report this or all of us could be reprimanded. That's the same stuff that happened to Penelope and Edythe. They knew what happened to us on line was wrong, but they went with it. They weren't strong enough to stand up against it, and now they're suspended just like Keisha and the rest of them fools. Well, baby, I'm not losing my letters. I worked too hard to get them. I thought you did too. I can't believe you did this. Dang!"

Then Bea got up and walked to the other side of the room. Trisha fell into my arms and sobbed even harder. I was so torn. I knew the right thing to do was to call the officials in our sorority right away to report all this. Yet, I also wanted to protect my friend. Either way, it was up to all of us to decide what to do, so we held a vote and decided to turn this in to Ms. Nixon.

I just hugged her tight and said, "We love you so much, and sometimes good people make bad decisions. Just because we're not going to stand behind your actions doesn't mean we're not standing behind you."

"But when you all turn me in, how is that standing behind me?" Trisha sobbed.

I touched her chin and said, "Girl, we are in college now. There are consequences for our actions. If you don't study for a test you get an F, you take money from the sorority and we got to report it. That doesn't mean we don't love you."

"Whatever, speak for yourself," Dena called out.

"Dena, come on girl," I said, hoping my soror would ease up from verbally kicking Trisha when she was down.

"No, because if I wouldn't have caught the discrepancy, I could have been kicked out of the sorority, or worse, gone to jail," Dena said.

She had a big point.

Trisha left my side and went to try and convince Dena to forgive her. "I'm sorry, Dena, I'm sorry. I just didn't see any other way to help myself."

Dena didn't respond. I nodded to Bea, who went over to her cell phone and dialed Ms. Berry instead of calling the Regional Coordinator.

"You calling her now?" Trisha said, with a trembling voice.

"Yeah, we got to report this now. We can't hold on to this information," I answered, completely wishing I didn't have to do this.

"This is going to ruin me. What if I go to jail? Please think about this," Trisha pleaded, as Bea ignored her and dialed.

"There is some kind of infraction code the sorority has," Sharon called out, remembering some of the information we had to memorize.

Sharon and a few others went over to find the discipline booklet and look up what was listed as a recommendation for this kind of offense. Bea came over and gave me the phone. All of this was so unfortunate. We'd just had Penelope, Keisha and all of the rest of our prophytes suspended. Now Alpha chapter was going to have more drama.

"So, your treasurer just got the checkbook and is already embezzling money?" Ms. Berry said to me.

"Yes ma'am," I said, quickly wanting this whole conversation to be over.

Ms. Berry said, "Well, you know being chapter president, you also have to sign each of the bank statements."

"One just came in. I was going to look at it, but I trusted Trisha had it under control. I have to do better."

"Yeah, you are going to have to do better. I'll call the Regional Coordinator now. We will get to the bottom of this."

Sharon came running over to me and said, "The booklet says that a person who steals money from the sorority will face a three-year suspension, a five hundred dollar fine, and they have to pay the money back."

"Well, Trisha isn't going to jail, right?" I said to Ms. Berry. "In the discipline code booklet, it gives a recommendation that's much lighter than that."

Ms. Berry said, "Yeah, but that's just a recommendation. You've got to send your own recommendation to the Regional Coordinator that your chapter has signed off on, and I've got to send one too. Then she makes her own judgment on whether to take this higher, and with all the trouble that Alpha chapter is already in, with a whole twenty or so girls suspended, she may be willing to throw the complete book at Trisha. She's in serious trouble. We won't get a final verdict on what will happen till next semester. All this takes a while."

Trisha saw the gloom on my face after speaking with Ms. Berry. She cried some more, as if our chapter wasn't broken enough. Here we were again, with more drama. Could we ever recover?

A month later, Sharon said, "So you the one who told us we been partying too much, but now you drag all of us to the Pi Lambda Beta Valentine's Day dance."

"Having to go through all those hearings and stuff over everything with Trisha, I figured y'all needed to come out and relax and release all that pent up frustration."

"Whatever," Bea said, giving me an eye like she had me pegged. "Hayden, you just wanted to come because you been dissing your boy."

Not wanting to entertain a discussion of her analysis, I said, "Dance, you guys, dance."

There were so many other sororities all over the place. We were so out-numbered because we had lost all the old heads. I couldn't even see my sisters when we split up. Then again, I really wasn't looking for them. I was looking for Creed. Bea had it right. I didn't want to try and find him by myself.

I missed my man. I had been so consumed with school and chapter drama, and catching up with my father, that I didn't spend enough time with Creed. Because I knew he was frustrated with me, it just seemed easier to keep my distance, even though deep in my heart that was far from what I wanted to do.

"Hey Chandra," I said to my roommate, as I bumped into her.

"Do I know you?" she turned and said to me sarcastically, letting me know I was no longer her favorite person.

"See, why are you trippin'?"

"I see you out at parties before I see you in our apartment. You're that busy that you can't call nobody and check on them, but now you gonna say, 'Hey,' all fake and phony. I should be leery of folks who treat me like you do."

"What do you mean leery?" I asked, getting a little offended. We weren't joined at the hip. Because I was busy didn't mean I didn't care.

"You're saying hey like we're tight. Like we're cool. Like we got a bond, and we don't have that. I'm going to treat you like you treat me. You don't deal with me at all, so see ya."

"Chandra, wait a minute," I said, totally not wanting our friendship to be over.

"Just like you lost a good man, you lost a good friend. I know you think you and your sorority sisters are all tight and everything, but word is going around that one of them took some money from y'all. If you left your wallet on my bed, I wouldn't take any of your money. But you chose to have a bond with a thief over the one we already had. You've completely put me down now that you're a Beta. Whatever girl, I hardly have time for it."

"It's not like that. Yeah, I got a lot of stuff going on, but you know I love you. I mean, I didn't think you were going to take it so personally," I said to my roommate.

"I didn't think you were going to diss me severely. When your girls don't show up you call me, but as long as they're around you can't manage to dial my number. I got severe issues with that," she said before walking away.

"Wait, Chandra, what do you mean I lost my man?"

"Girl, I just saw him over by the restroom, hemmed up with some MEM, lockin' lips in a serious way. I thought you were the one who called it off. Heck, you been spending all your time with them girls. I didn't know if you swung another way or something."

Rolling my eyes, I huffed, "Oh see, Chandra, you didn't even need to go there with me."

"I'm just saying you lost your boy."

And then she was gone for real. I didn't know if she was pulling my chain just to annoy me or what. However, I walked to the restroom where she said she had seen Creed. I stopped dead in my tracks when I saw him with gorgeous Tammy Knight, the MEM chapter president. I was stunned by their display of affection. His tongue was in her ear.

Part of me wanted to slide in between them and say,

"Excuse me, what the heck is going on? Get your crusty, yucky lips off of my guy." But seeing how much he was enjoying himself, I knew I would be embarrassed. If I couldn't even make Chandra understand that though I had been absent, it wasn't because I didn't care, I knew there was no way Creed would understand. I guess that's what hurt the most, because even though I wasn't with him, it wasn't like I was dying to get with another guy. He was so into Tammy, he didn't even realize I was standing there.

Lord, where did I go wrong? I asked.

I couldn't take it anymore, I had to find Bridget. When I spotted her, she was with some of her other MEM friends, but I didn't care. I tugged on her arm and pulled her over to a corner.

"Ouch," she said, hitting my hand. "What's going on? Why you want to embarrass me like that?"

"How you gonna let your president get with my man?"

"Everybody has been teasing her for a couple weeks because she likes underclassmen, but she said he was the hottest thing on the line and she just wants him."

"And you didn't tell her he was with your roommate?"

"We're roommates? Myra, Chandra, and I haven't even had dinner together lately. We have all been in our own separate worlds. You have been too. I figured that if you were doing your job, Tammy wouldn't be able to take him, and if she did catch him, you wouldn't want him anymore. I stayed out of it. You're a big girl. Why would I get in all that mess and cause more drama?"

"Because I thought you were loyal to me."

"Like you would help an MEM over a BGP, girl please,"

Bridget said to me, shoving me aside. "Plus, Tammy is my prophyte. What was I going to tell her?" she said, hoping I'd understand her plight.

"I guess that's just it, Bridget. Anything would've been better than nothing. Thanks for staying out of it. I lost the only guy I ever cared for." I could not hold back the tears from dripping down my face.

She shrugged her shoulders. I guess we were just at that point in our relationship where it was clear things weren't what they used to be. Not only had I lost Creed and Chandra, but it looked like Bridget too.

As I walked away from Bridget, Dena came over and grabbed my arm. "Girl, you've gotta come see this."

"I'm ready to leave. I want to get out of this place."

"No, Bea's about to fight."

"What!" I said, emotionally not able to take another thing.

"Yes, and with your man."

I was so confused. "I don't understand."

"Come here, come on."

Dena took me back around the corner where I had seen Creed with Tammy.

"You suppose to be with my homegirl and you gonna be with this chick," Bea said to him.

"I know you not about to put your hand all up in my face," Tammy said, sporting an ultra sheer pink mini-dress.

"It is an unspoken rule—when a man is taken, all the rest of the folks in sorority land stay back. You don't want the war to be on, now do you?" Bea said to Tammy fearlessly.

"Girl, looking at you and your oversized behind, I don't think any of my sorors would have to worry about you taking their man." Tammy lifted her nose at Bea. "And if your girl was doing her job, this one wouldn't be free for me to take in the first place."

"Come on, let's get out of here," Creed said to Tammy.

"No, you hold up," Bea said, pushing him back.

"Wait a minute now, you need to get your hands off me. I ain't trying to hit no girl, but dang, Hayden had her chance. She was more into working with y'all than she was into keeping me happy. So I'm staying out of the way. I found someone who can manage running a chapter *and* giving me love," Creed said harshly.

Just hearing all that hurt so bad.

"Yo' drunk behind need to go sit down and think about what you talking about," Bea said, as she got a whiff of his breath.

He was drunk? It didn't matter, I knew when people were intoxicated what they really thought came out. Creed was hurt and he wasn't waiting anymore. I put him to the side for two months and that was two months too long.

I went over to Bea and said, "Girl, thanks, but this ain't your fight."

"If it hurts you, I'm in it." She hit my back.

My eyes were teary—this was truly affecting me. Creed licked his lips and faced me for the first time that night. Knowing that I knew he had moved on, he didn't appear broken.

I collected all the strength I could muster and uttered, "Bea, he's where he wants to be. I'm cool with that. I don't want no beef with the MEMs. Tammy's right. She couldn't take what was really mine."

"But Hayden, all you do is talk about Creed. You dragged us here so you could be with him. You wanted tonight to be the . . ."

I placed my hand over her mouth and said, "Come on, let's go."

Creed attempted to follow me, but Tammy held him back. Alcohol or not, broken heart or not, it was right for us to be apart. Dena and Bea took me into the ladies' room.

Unable to stop the tears, I said, "I'm not going to let this get to me, y'all. I'm fine, it's okay."

"Dang girl, I know we're high maintenance, but you can't be losing your guy," Bea said, getting me a tissue.

"Yeah, Creed was the hottest thing on that line. Shoot, he's smart too. Everybody's talking about him. We been telling everybody he was yours and nobody made a move."

"I appreciate the loyalty, but we're all young, trying to find our way. I'm just a sophomore in college. What excites me today doesn't hold my attention tomorrow. Obviously, that's the same thing going on with him. Good riddance, you know. How would it look for the Beta Gamma Pi president to be crying over some dude? Tah, whatever," I said to them, going to the mirror and wiping my face.

Bea came over and looked at my reflection. "Ain't nothing wrong with letting us know you are hurt. Yeah, you are the leader, but you're human."

"I hear you girl, but I'm alright."

I walked out of the bathroom and was surprised to bump into Butch, my former boyfriend, who also happened to be a Pi.

"Dang girl, that dress is fitting you mighty fine. I love you in lavender. Can I have this dance?" he said, almost drooling.

"Yeah," I said, not really understanding why I let the jerk usher me out onto the dance floor. He slid his hand from my back to my bottom. Though I tried to tug away, he eased me back to him.

"I knew it was only a matter of time before I got you back in my arms," he said, with breath so bad I personally wanted to run to the drug store and buy up every bottle of Scope to give to him.

The song couldn't end soon enough for me. When I tried to pull away, we both saw Creed's eyes plastered on us.

Creed came onto the dance floor and said, "What's all this? You letting him touch you all out here and everything."

"You can't have your cake and eat it too, Creed," I said.

"Yeah, step back, man," Butch told him.

"Man, take your hands off of her," he said to Butch.

"Everybody in here knows you just dissed her. Everybody is out here looking. Don't get jealous because I got what you really want."

"Oh, so it's like that, Hayden? For real?" he had the nerve to ask me.

With Butch's hand on my waist, I placed my hand over his, smiled and said to Creed, "Is that a problem?"

BREAKDOWN

$\mathcal{L}$ooking at my grades, I freaked. "I don't know what I'm gonna do, Bea. My mom is going to kill me!"

"Parents don't see progress reports, girl."

"I know, but two Bs and two Cs? She was ticked off when I went from a 4.0 to a 3.6. I gotta get it together."

"You get your head out of that rituals book, wake up and start studying some school books, you'll bring your grades up. Everybody's been telling you to multitask, but you don't, Hayden. It's like you're taking this president thing so seriously. I'm your first vice and you won't even let me help you do anything."

"Alright, alright. It just seems like ever since I took office, we haven't been able to stand on our own two feet. If we're not knocked down to our knees, we're hobbling around on one leg, trying to act like we got it all together."

"I still can't believe you convinced the chapter sorors

to do outside fundraisers to help Trisha pay back her debt."

"I mean, what was the alternative? Did you really want her to go to jail?"

"Speaking of people that should be in jail—look, there's Keisha walking toward us."

"Exactly. She's still walking free and she almost killed somebody. Trisha should be able to have a second chance too."

"Alright, I hear you."

"Move over," Keisha said to us as if we were supposed to split the sidewalk and let her pass.

"I ain't on your line no more, trick," Bea said to her, just as grumpy.

"What? Somebody want a beat down?" Keisha said, pushing Bea in the chest.

"Guys, we're still sorority sisters. Why we gotta act like this?" I said to the two of them, knowing I was basically talking to myself because they looked at me like I was on drugs.

"I'm not sorority sisters with y'all. Y'all don't even know how to run a yard."

"What are you talking about?" Bea asked her.

"Look over there right now. Look at our rock. Look at our benches and look who's walking through it like they don't have no respect," Keisha said.

"So, people can't walk on our stuff?" I asked her. I really wanted her opinion about this because this was something nobody schooled us on.

"Do you walk through the Rho Tau Nu or the MEMs property?" she asked me.

"My classes aren't that way," I said.

"Well look over there at their side. The MEMs have someone manning their rock at all times. During the day they rotate somebody so folks don't just stroll through. No one is watching our property and we're getting no respect."

"But there's stuff that you thought we should know," Bea said. "Why can't you just be a woman and tell us? You don't have to try and diss anybody. It's not our fault that y'all got kicked out."

"Whatever. Y'all were too weak to handle the small little pressure we were putting on you. I can't help if y'all don't have any real leadership. Y'all doing so much stuff wrong, it's pathetic. Founders' Day is coming up on March nineteenth. Y'all have anything cool planned for the Beta Rock? And every day this month we're supposed to do something special. We ain't even seen no service projects from y'all. And from what I hear, your grades are slippin'," she said, looking at me. "President and first vice couldn't even make sure that they kept their treasurer girlfriend in check. Yeah, y'all are pathetic and definitely not my sisters. Move!"

"Oh no she—"

"Just come on," I said to Bea, before she said or did something we'd regret. "Let her go."

"Well, I'm sick of people thinking just because we don't know everything that they can treat us any kind of way. Them MEM girls know not to walk all up in our space. If they didn't do it last year, then why they disrespecting us now?" Bea saw Bridget walking toward our rock. "See, I'm about to cut her off right now. Hold my books."

"Bea wait! That's my—" Before I knew it, she was gone.

Why did this have to be a brawl between sororities? Everyone has their favorite, and honestly, though I prefer Beta Gamma Pi, all the sororities have good points. We didn't need to create any beef with anyone. I certainly didn't need my soror going at it with my roommate.

I rushed over to our rock and heard Bea say, "You need to take your little self around the path. Y'all know you're not supposed to walk all through our stuff. We don't do that to you."

"Don't blow this out of proportion. I'm just trying to get to class," Bridget said, calmly.

"I'm just sick and tired of all these other sororities on campus trying to act like because our prophytes aren't on the yard no more, they can dog us out and laugh behind our back. We are still a part of the Alpha chapter. That's right, everybody, the Betas are in the house!"

"You are making a fool out of yourself," I said to Bea. "Calm down!"

"You better get your girl," Bridget said to me.

"Bea, go on and go to class. I'ma stay here for a minute, alright? Go to class!"

"Hayden, you are the one that needs to be going to class. You're the one sayin' your grades are slippin'. Don't get mad because I'm not scared of none of these fools standing around here. You say you wanna be a leader, but then you act all pitiful when one of your little roommates comes around. Forget her."

"Forget you!" Bridget said, as Bea stomped off.

The two of us were left standing there. It was really

sort of awkward. We'd been avoiding each other in the house. When I knew she was in the kitchen, I'd stay in my room. Thankfully, we each had our own restrooms, so I didn't need to mix with any of my roommates for any reason other than to use the kitchen.

"Really, Hayden," she said, breaking the silence. "I didn't know that this was taboo, but none of my sisters told anybody on my line. You guys are never here. I'm just trying to get to class and this is the quickest way. I wasn't trying to show any disrespect. You know that's not in my nature. You know that, right?" she said.

"Yeah, I know. It's just been really hard," I said, sitting down on a bench. "I'm failing at everything."

Putting aside Greek partisanship, my dear old friend sat down beside me and said, "Girl, it is just not that serious."

"Uh, we're probably breaking protocol right now; an MEM and a Beta having a conversation on my sorority's bench. If my prophytes don't want you to walk through here, they certainly don't want me practically inviting you over to sit and break bread. So I can't do anything right," I said, as Bridget stood up to leave. "No please, I don't want you to go anywhere. I miss you."

"I miss you too. And just so you know, Creed dumped my chapter president, Tammy. She told me she didn't have time for it anyway because she really thought he was still hung up on you."

For the first time in a long time, I kind of smiled. A couple of weeks had passed since the whole Valentine's Day dance fiasco. As hard as I tried to get Creed off my mind, I still knew deep down I was hurt we were over.

"He hasn't called me, girl. That night at their party, I embarrassed him, so I know we're through."

"You're a smart girl though, Hayden. You'll figure out a way to get back up. Before you know it everything will be right again."

I gave her the biggest hug and we kept talking while walking straight through the MEM block, not caring about what anybody else thought. Friendship was friendship. And ours was really true. It couldn't be broken.

Later in the week, I was just getting home from class, when I opened the front door and saw Chandra, Bridget and Myra were all sitting at the dinner table talking and laughing. Whatever one of them had cooked smelled so good and I was so hungry. I missed our time together, so putting my pride aside, I put my stuff down and walked toward the dinner table.

"Hey y'all," I said, looking pitiful.

"Hey!" Myra said. "You hungry?"

I looked over at the stove. There was turkey and collard greens. I wanted some badly.

Myra said, "Macaroni and cheese, gravy and dressing are over there too. You're welcome to some if you want."

"What's this? Thanksgiving? You threw down!" I said, quickly going over and grabbing a plate.

Myra said, "Yeah, I just felt like we needed some bonding time. Didn't think you were gonna make it, but it's good to have you in the house."

"Yeah, I'm glad you're here," Bridget said.

I could hear Bridget kicking Chandra under the table. Because Chandra and I were so close, she held me most accountable for being out of touch. Myra and Bridget understood a little more because they pledged as well.

Chandra nonchalantly voiced, "Whatever. If she wanna sit, she can sit."

"Bridget was telling us that you guys talked the other day," Myra said, making small talk.

When I sat down, I bowed my head. I needed to pray, but I also didn't want to deal with tough questions and heavy conversation. I just wanted to eat! So after my long prayer, I hoped she had forgotten her question.

When I didn't say anything, Myra said to Bridget, "This is gonna be so exciting. Rho Tau Nu and the MEMs doing a service project together. I know this is really going to make an impact."

I listened as the two of them talked. They were so happy about this collaborative project. Of course the green-eyed monster arose from within me, and it wasn't from chugging down the collard greens. I couldn't understand why they hadn't asked me and my sorority to be a part of it.

Chandra chimed in and said, "Out of all the things you guys do, a voter registration drive is completely something I'm for. The presidential election is coming up in November and too many college kids aren't even registered. We've got power and don't even use it. I'll spread the word on campus of where you guys will be signing folks up."

They just kept talking around me and though I was eating the delicious meal, I wanted our old friendhsip back. So putting aside all the barriers, I said, "I owe y'all a big apology. And I guess I never thought it would be hard for me to say this, but I'm really sorry."

"For what?" Chandra said.

"For everything. Being a jerk, walking away from you guys, being consumed by everything but the things that are most important."

"Well nobody's saying that you leading a sorority isn't important," Bridget said.

"Well, I was saying that!" Chandra added.

"Girl," Bridget said, taking her napkin and popping Chandra with it.

"No for real, we've all been busy," Myra said. "But we gotta make time for this. Whether we're in a sorority or not, it should never break up this bond."

"Yeah, because I befriended some girls that honestly I didn't really know," I said. "And I have been hurt in trusting some of them."

"You wanna talk about it?" Bridget asked me.

"Naw, I just need y'all to pray for me. But I really would like to be a part of this whole joint service project I'm hearing you talk about."

"Really? You think the Betas would want to be a part of it?" Myra said, doubt written all across her face.

"I know we seem like we don't have our act together, but yeah," I said in an excited tone.

"You probably want to talk to them about it first," Bridget said.

"I'm the president. I don't need to talk to them. When is it?"

"Tomorrow," Myra said.

"And y'all didn't talk to me about it? Y'all didn't even think about us?"

"Girl, we hadn't been able to catch up with you," Myra said to me.

"Alright, alright," I said.

Myra stood and said, "But I know it would be great to have the Betas on board. I'll call my president to check."

"And I'll do the same with mine," Bridget said.

"And I'll send out a mass e-mail to my sorors," I said, "giving them all the details once you both get the okay."

After getting clearance from the RTNs and MEMs, excitement ran all through my veins. As a leader this was something great. Getting the Betas connected with other sororities is huge. We had little riffs here and there, but this would squash all of that. With this project, we'd have a chance to collectively do something for the greater good of the university, while getting our voice back.

However, the next day all my excitement about us participating vanished when again, I was the only one who showed up at the event. Girls from both the other organizations had most of their chapter members present. The girls were nice to me, but I was embarrassed.

Livid, I called an emergency meeting at our room on campus and all of them heifers showed up instantly. "I just don't understand. Where were y'all? You say you care about our name. You say you want to make a difference. But yet, anytime I need y'all to be there ain't none of y'all around. But let me call an emergency meeting and everybody's here. Y'all love the drama. All you guys seem to care about is partying and getting all up in folks' faces and goin' off on them. What about showing up to give back?"

"Wait a minute," Bea said. "When I got up in Creed and Bridget's face, I was trying to have your back."

"Well, if you recall, Bea, on the line I had yours, okay?"

"Hey, hold up now, Hayden, that's the whole problem. You've been reading up on the rituals on how to be leader, but you haven't been practicing what you preach. You sign us up for stuff but you don't even talk to us about it. I had class, so I couldn't go. How could you not ask us?" Dena said.

Sharon said, "I was committed to a study group."

"So see, it wasn't like we didn't want to be there, but we had other things that we were committed to. You can't give us a few hours notice and expect us to just be there at your beck and call. You're our chapter president, not our dictator. And as you can see, you don't have as much power as you think."

I couldn't even stay in the room with them. I picked up my purse and slammed the door. This was crazy.

I hated that I had to park so far across campus. I couldn't find a close parking spot before the meeting, and now it was starting to drizzle, so I started to run.

Once I got my jog on, I actually felt free. The tears mixed with the rain liberated me. I was having my own personal pity party and nobody could tell. No one was around me, so they couldn't see the inner turmoil that I was going through.

But then across campus by the entrance of the psychology building, I saw a familiar face having way too much fun. My professor of psychology was hugging and kissing a lady. As I got closer, I was surprised to see it was my uncle's wife! It made absolutely no sense to me why she would be kissing a man that wasn't my uncle.

Already upset and full of emotion, I had to make sure

she didn't lay her lips on him for one more second. But before I got too close, I thought about it all. I mean, Dr. Griffin was my professor, and I hadn't done so well in his psych class. Maybe if he saw me, he'd be forced to change my C into an A.

What was I thinking? This wasn't about me. This was about my uncle. This was his wife.

"Hey Auntie, what's going on?" I said, catching her completely off guard. She immediately pulled away from my professor.

"Hey Doc," I said to him.

"Hey, you're one of my students, right?" He managed to muster.

Setting the record straight, I pointed a reprimanding finger at them and said, "Yeah, there's not that many students in the class. You know she's married to my uncle, the president of this school, right? What's going on here?"

"Hayden, this isn't the time," my trifling aunt said.

"Oh no, it's not what it looked like," he added quickly.

"What are you saying? It's exactly what it looked like," she said.

I couldn't believe that the two of them went from kissing each other to arguing about their *relationship* right in front of me. Thankfully this was just the medicine I needed to get over all the drama I was dealing with.

"Don't look at me that way, Anna. I'm not trying to lose my job over this. You're not gonna tell your uncle, right?" he asked me.

"She's not gonna say anything. She doesn't know what she saw."

"You can't tell me what I'm gonna say," I snapped.

"Just leave, Drew. I've got this," she said to my professor. Now I knew his first name.

"Seriously, I've got a wife and three kids at home. I need my job," he pleaded.

I said, "So you're not just gonna destroy my uncle with this little thing the two of you got going on here. You don't care about destroying the lives of your wife and children?"

"Stay out of this, Hayden. Nobody cares about the soap opera you're making out of this," she said.

"Oh no, Doc here definitely cares. He teaches it. It's not what people do, but it's about the reasons behind their choices that make the world go round. Isn't what you're doing going to have consequences that can never be fixed?" I asked him.

"Anna, just talk to her. I got to get home. I knew this was a bad idea," he said, putting his briefcase over his head to cover himself from the rain as he ran to his car.

When she and I were alone, she said, "How dare you come up to me threatening to tell your uncle. I am a grown woman!"

"Yes, and you're his wife. Does he know what you're doing?"

"We have some things that we keep from each other, it's *our* marriage. You have no business in it, no place in it. So stay out of it."

"I'll let him tell me that," I said to her.

"You just don't understand, Hayden. Things have been going south for us for a very long time."

"I walked in on you practically beating him a couple of months back and I overlooked that. My mom said he's been miserable, and I just thought it was marriage pains, but this, what you just did, I can't ignore."

"You and your mom are such busybodies. She doesn't know what she's talking about. He always compares me to your mom, his perfect little sister."

"She's his older sister. That's just it. You never got to know our family."

"Well regardless of what you think about me, your uncle is happy."

"He sure didn't look happy when you were trying to strangle him in his office," I said to her.

How dumb did she think I was? Like I wasn't going to tell him. As soon as I left her, I was going to squeal like a mouse.

"You can't tell your uncle, you just can't!" she said, grabbing my arm, trying to be sincere with me.

"Please don't tell me what I can and can't do. And let my arm go," I said to her. "Now!"

"No Hayden, you can't. You gotta hear me out. You have everything. You're young, beautiful, intelligent, and in a good college. You just got into the sorority you wanted to join all your life. Don't take away the one thing that I need. Let me keep my marriage. Please don't say anything, Hayden. If you make me lose him, I don't know what I'll do. I might have a breakdown."

14

GUSHING

"**P**lease, you've got to get off of me," I said to my uncle's wife.

I couldn't think of her as my aunt. Actually, I never had. She always seemed to be so stuffy. She never gave me a hug, not that I could remember. But now she stood there clinging to my arm, begging me not to destroy her.

"Does the fact that I just poured my heart out to you mean anything? I know you're just going to go and tell him anyway. Well, thanks for nothing," she said, stepping out into the pouring rain.

Alright Lord, what would You do? She's stepping outside of her marriage. How could I live with myself if I don't tell my uncle the truth? I mean blood is thicker than mud, right. I don't even know why I'm having second thoughts about this. Could I be a horrible person if I don't tell him? Show me what to do. Show me how to have the right spirit about this. Don't let me just act out in vengeance because I never really liked my aunt in the first place. And please don't let me react because I am miserable right now in my own life.

As I prayed, I found myself going toward my uncle's office. I figured if I wasn't supposed to be there something would happen to stop me. But there was no divine intervention.

"Hey Hayden, does your uncle know you're coming?" his secretary said, in the friendliest voice I had heard all day.

"No, but if he's busy, I can come back another time. I just had a moment and needed to talk to him, but it's okay, it's no big deal. You don't need to bother him." *What am I doing?* I was now having second thoughts, but before I could go anywhere his secretary quickly picked up the phone and buzzed him.

"Okay, I'll tell her," she said, as she hung up. "He's ready to see you. Before you go in I don't want you to get the impression that you have to call first, because you never do. Anytime you need to see him, your uncle will squeeze you in. It's just last time was awkward."

I took a deep sigh, as I entered his office. I was torn as to whether I should tell him what I had just witnessed.

"Hey girl, give me a hug," he said. "The wife and I were trying to get over there for Christmas, but we just didn't get a chance to come see you guys. Now it's March. I talk to your sister more than I do you. Crazy, when you and I share the same space practically. What in the world is going on with that?"

"Life, it's busy. I don't mean to take up any more of your time. I just came by to say hi. Let me go."

"No, no girl. You never just come by to say hi. Sit. I have a refrigerator over here full of Coke. I'm sure you want a cup?"

"You still remember my favorite drink?"

"Yep, and I got a few, hoping you would come by."

I looked all around his office and saw all of his pictures. There was a picture of me and my sister, but mostly the pictures were of him and his wife. As I sat there chugging the Coke he set on his desk for me, he went on and on about the promotion she just got. She was a drugstore manager and now she was going to be managing several stores in Little Rock. I wasn't impressed at all.

He said, "I'm just so proud of her. She is the light of my life. The last time you came in here, I know it was kind of an awkward situation."

"That was months ago and I truly don't think your marriage is getting better," I said from nowhere.

He leaned forward and said, "What are you talking about?"

I knew what I had to do. I had to tell him the truth. He seemed so blind to all that was going on around him. I just couldn't have him live that way anymore.

Cutting through the uneasiness, I said, "I just saw your wife with one of my professors."

"She was on campus with a teacher?" The confused look he gave me urged me to divulge more.

However, I needed him to think this through. It just didn't make sense she was somewhere where she had no business being, with a person that she wasn't supposed to be with. I could tell by his expression he connected the dots without any help from me.

"I'm sorry, I just love you too much," I said, seeing the despair rise over his usually strong and upbeat face.

He nodded, went over to his door and opened it. I knew he needed time alone so I just got up and kissed him on the forehead and hoped and prayed that I did the right thing. Truth was always good, wasn't it?

When I left his office, I checked my cell phone and saw that I had five missed calls from Sharon, then Dena, Sharon again, Bea and then Audria.

There was also a text from Bea: We're still in the meeting room. Come back.

"So Bea, you want me to come back?" I said aloud. "I knew it!"

I felt pretty good about myself. How did they not think they owed their leader an apology? They should have done whatever I told them to do. It was for their own good.

When I got back to the meeting room, all the smiles I thought I would see and all the apologies I thought I would hear were replaced with something I was not expecting.

"About time you came back," Bea said, like I was her worst enemy. "We've been waiting here forever, like we ain't got other stuff to do."

"I had to get myself together and go see my uncle, okay. Some things came up on my end too," I replied, a little on the defensive.

"Alright, well can you have a seat, Hayden," Sharon said. "Please don't take this the wrong way, but . . ."

"I don't care how she takes it," Bea interrupted.

"Take what? What is all of this about? Just let all of the hot feelings subside. I thought that is what y'all had done, but obviously I was wrong. Why don't we just talk tomorrow?"

Bea insisted, "Naw, we can't talk tomorrow, sister, sit down like Sharon said. We talking today."

"Okay, then talk," I said as I sat down.

Bea looked at Sharon. Sharon looked at Dena. Dena looked at the other girls in the room and they all looked back at Bea.

"Alright, well I'll just tell her. We think . . ."

"No, I'll say it," Sharon said. "You ain't got to be so mean, girl. She is supposed to be your girl and you just gonna blurt it out?"

"Blurt what out?" I demanded.

"We just don't think you're fit to be our president anymore. The way you see things in running this chapter isn't the way the majority of us want it," Sharon said.

"What majority? The few of y'all against the rest of us?" I said, really hoping most of my line sisters hadn't turned on me for real.

Bea said, "No, fourteen of us against you."

"I don't get what I've done that's so crazy for you guys to feel that y'all don't want me to be the chapter president anymore."

I had given up so much for them. My grades were slipping. I didn't have a man anymore. I hadn't been keeping in touch with my family. I even had beef with my room-mates. All because every single ounce of energy I had was poured into Beta Gamma Pi, Alpha Chapter. And now they were telling me they didn't want me to be their leader. Them chicks had to be on crack and I was the only one in my right mind.

"I know this is a shock," Sharon said, trying to come over and console me. "I know you cared about your position."

Moving away from her phony hug, I said, "I don't care about my position. Being president is one thing, but I care about you guys. I care about this chapter."

"But ever since you have been president things haven't been that great," Dena said.

Audria chimed in, "And I've just been praying."

"Audria, you're not the only one who prays, okay."

"I'm just saying, because I know this is going to be hard, Hayden, but sometimes you've got to just step aside. We love you as a soror, we just don't want you as a president. It's not like we're trying to kick you out of the chapter or anything."

Inside, I was bawling, but no tears would fall. I guess the rain had washed them all away. I just didn't want them to see me crack.

"So tell us how we go about it." Bea stood over me and asked, "Do we just raise our hands and you're not the president anymore? We didn't want to do this without you. It's not like we voted or anything yet, so tell us what we need to do."

I had been studying protocol. I knew the procedure for handling this. But it wasn't like I was going to give them the ammunition to take me down.

"You're not the only one who can give us the information," Bea continued when I remained silent. "We do have an advisor."

"And all of these little meetings we had without her," I said, so they knew I knew, "have been totally out of order anyway."

"Then that's another reason why we need to get you out. You're the one acting all in charge, calling emergency meetings left and right and demanding that we be places. Getting us to take *our* time to spend on a girl who stole from us, I mean what kind of leader are you?"

"Alright!" Sharon said to Bea.

"I just want to make sure she gets the point. We're all completely fed up with her. We need to do something about it right now."

"If that's the way you feel about it, Bea, then do what you got to do. There is no need for me to fight you. I can see the avalanche falling down the mountainside and I'm not trying to be rolled over. I can get out of the way." I didn't really want to move on, but as Audria says, "Sometimes you pray about it and leave it in God's hands." I knew I had done my best and obviously that wasn't good enough. So now He needed to decide my fate and I had to be okay with it. So I left, for good, that day.

For two days, I stayed in my room. I didn't go to class, I didn't take any calls. I barely put anything in my stomach. I just wanted to be left alone. I didn't feel great and before I could find a way to get along with my sorority sisters, I had to find a way to get along with myself.

"Hey lady, do you mind if I come in?" Bridget said, standing outside my door.

"No Bridg. Girl, I'm fine," I said, in an unconvincing tone.

"Hayden, open up the door please," she said.

I wanted to crawl under the covers and be left alone. When she knocked again, I knew she really cared, so I went over to the door and unlocked it.

"I know I look a mess. I did brush my teeth though and don't look at my room. I know you're a neat freak," I said.

"I wasn't trying to be presumptuous," she said, "but . . ."

"What did you do? Please don't tell me you called my momma?"

"No, but I did talk to my chapter president."

"What? You called the girl that was dating Creed? Are you kidding me?" I asked, totally ticked off.

"Well, your friend does care about you deeply," Tammy said, as she stepped slowly into my view.

"Well, that's okay. I don't need counseling, particularly from a MEM."

"Yeah, I know so I called my good friend," Tammy said, and she yanked on someone behind her wearing a lavender shirt.

I looked perplexed. I didn't know what she was talking about. And in walked Penelope.

"We were roommates when we were on line," Penelope said to me, pointing to Bridget's big sister. "But as you know I made the smarter choice, or so I thought before I got kicked out of the sorority. But some bonds go deeper than that."

Tammy said, "Penelope has been following Alpha chapter, and cares about y'all, even as she sits on the outs. You guys talk."

"If you want me to go, I'll leave," Penelope said, not trying to force me into talking.

"No. Come in please," I said, knowing maybe this was a blessing.

The MEMs left my room. I shut the door and pulled my chair from my desk for her to sit. Penelope sat down and looked firmly into my eyes.

I said, "Thanks for coming. I thought everyone had abandoned me."

"I understand that feeling, but even when I was kicked out, you came over and said something that really stuck with me."

"What did I say?" I asked, unsure of what that could be.

"You said you cared. And I have always cared about you. I'm sure I let you down as leader of the line, but it's hard being a leader of anything."

"Well, I certainly know that now. I never knew there was such a thing as caring too much, and now they don't want me to lead them at all. It's clear that I don't know what I'm doing."

"And I didn't either, but I have had a lot of time for reflection. Wondering why I couldn't stand up to Keisha and have her take a step back when she was going too far. My leadership or lack of it allowed her to take me down, you know?"

"Yeah!" I replied. "So what you're saying is that even though we may have the right motives, we just didn't go about it the right way." Penelope nodded in agreement.

"But how can I change that? How can I make it better? I'm so confused. Ever since I walked out, I feel like I failed myself, because that isn't me, I am the kind of person that wants the best for everybody. I'm not selfish, I'm not demanding, I . . ." I could not even finish my sentence. Realizing that I really didn't know myself at all, I was speechless.

"The way that you see yourself is from your point of view. But when you see it from someone else's side, it makes you come at it from a different angle."

"Well, how can I lead right? How can I care? Or let them know that I do? I mean I just want to have a little bit of everyone in me, you know? Keisha and Bea are so strong, even Sharon is so likeable and smart."

"But you've got to be you. You've got to do it your way. You've got to let your heart guide you. You've got to work what you've got."

"I keep hearing that," I said.

"Hayden, you can't just demand that they keep you on as their president, nor can you make them follow you. But you certainly can talk to them in a way to make them *want* to follow you. To make them believe you care about what is right for them. I know there is no better president for this chapter than you, Hayden Grant, but you have to find your own place."

It was amazing to me, within the past forty-eight hours I tried to find some kind of direction, some kind of way to pick up the pieces and let out all that was pent up inside. Now, I could really feel the bond of sisterhood, because a girl that had been cast out had come back to let me know she still was on her job, she wasn't going to let me go.

"I love Beta Gamma Pi, Hayden. Even with my gems taken, I love Beta Gamma Pi. That means I love you, my sister."

Penelope's open heart meant the world to me. I got up and hugged her, as we cried tears of joy, blessed to feel the real bond of sisterhood. It felt great not being phony and holding back. We cared, and those feelings came gushing out.

PRIORITY

"Momma, I'm not going to Founders' Day, so quit asking me, okay. Please leave it alone and don't tell me that I have to go," I said to her over the phone as I lay across my bed.

A big hole was already in my heart, knowing that this was my first Founders' Day as a member of Beta Gamma Pi. While we were on the line we only read about how moving and significant Founders' Day celebrations were. It's an event that the collegiate chapters host in conjunction with the alumnae chapters. All we had to do was show up, and because I hadn't talked to my line sisters in days, I had no idea if they were going to attend or not. Since they hadn't reached out to me, I knew they didn't even care if I was going, and that hurt.

"Hayden, I understand you're tired and your studies may be weighing you down, but as Chapter President there are some responsibilities you just cannot walk away from," my mom insisted.

I hadn't felt the need to call her and let her know that I was asked to step down as Chapter President. I was too embarrassed. What was I going to say, "Oh Mom, your little girl that you think is so great isn't that great at all?"

"What's going on, Hayden, talk to me girl. My Chapter President called me and asked me when was the last time I talked to you. Now is there something going on out there in the world of Beta Gamma Pi that I need to be aware of? Remember, I've been a member of the organization for almost two decades. I ran for a lot of positions, got a few of them and lost a lot of them. I know there can be a dark side to this sisterhood."

I never thought that she could understand what I was feeling, but when she put it that way, maybe she could. I remember when she ran for Regional Coordinator and lost to the woman who is now the National President. I know that she often thinks about how things would be different if she would have won years back. Maybe she would be National President now. How cool would that have been for me? My mom heading the organization that I loved so dearly. But, it didn't work out that way, and though she lost, she still remained active. She didn't hide, she didn't quit. What did she have that allowed her to keep going when she felt broken?

So I said, "Okay, Mom, I didn't want to let you down, so that's why I haven't told you this."

"Told me what, sweetie? Please talk to me."

"A couple weeks ago I had a big run-in with . . ."

"I know, your uncle called me. He told me all about you seeing his wife out and all that and I just left you alone because I knew that had to be hard, going to him. Baby, you did the right thing."

"No Mom, I'm not talking about that, though I didn't tell you about it because it wasn't my business. I figured if Uncle Wade wanted you to know, he would tell you himself."

"Okay, I respect that."

"Great."

"So what's going on?"

"It's related to the sorority. Actually, it was that same day. My line sisters called a meeting. When I showed up they all decided that I wasn't the one they wanted to lead them anymore."

"Oh Hayden, are you serious, honey?" she said in a deflated tone.

"Yes ma'am," I said, thankful that she showed some sympathy. She didn't just brush this under the rug and tell me everything was okay.

"So who's the new president?" she asked.

"I don't even know. I left before all of that was decided. They haven't called me, I haven't called them. I've only spoken to the old First Vice President—"

"Penelope?" My mom asked, interrupting me.

"Yes ma'am."

"Oh, I've always liked that girl."

"You really know her?"

"Yeah, when she was pledging a couple years back, I was working with the line. She just had such character."

"Well, she came over and talked to me. I've been

thinking a lot about what she said, but I don't know how to make it better. If Founders' Day is on our campus, I can't be there, I can't show up. I just don't want to deal with any craziness."

"Well sweetheart, that is one of the reasons I didn't want you to pledge because you would get to see some of the ugliness that goes on. Trust me, I am not saying you did everything right, they may even be justified in telling you to hit the road."

"Mom!" I said, needing her to be on my side.

"Nor was I saying they were right, but despite all that there is a way you work things out with your sorority sisters. You pledged not because you wanted to be Chapter President but because you wanted to be a part of the organization. You vowed to help make it better. Sitting on the sidelines, Hayden, will not accomplish that goal. You've got to face your sorority sisters. You can't back down from what you signed up to be a part of. Get dressed. I will be over there in thirty minutes. I'm on my way."

"Mom, I didn't buy a ticket," I said, hoping she'd leave me alone.

"Hayden, you know my chapter doesn't ask you girls to buy tickets."

"Oh yeah, that's right," I said, completely not thinking, wanting an excuse.

"One day you will know how it felt to run for regional office and get defeated. I had support going in, major support, but there was a big scandal thrown from the other candidate and I got ousted. Though I wanted to crawl into a hole and hide, I knew I couldn't. The only way to get better, the only way to give what I said I was going to give to the organization, the only way to make it change for the positive was to stay involved. That was my number one reason for signing up and that was the number one thing that kept me in when I wanted to quit. Keep that at the forefront of your mind and no one can make you turn away. I'll see you in a sec. Love you."

Before I could plead with my mom to let me stay home, she'd already hung up. I knew she was on her way. I had to find a black outfit to wear in honor of our founders and get dressed quickly because when she honked she would be expecting me to head out the door. I loved her persistence, her stamina, her care for me. I just needed her to lighten up sometimes and I really felt this was one of those times. Though she made a great argument about why I needed to get myself out of hibernation, this was hard.

When my mom got there, Chandra ran out to the car first. She always had my back when it came to that. She knew my mom could be a little high maintenance, and she occupied her by saying hello and catching her up on all that had been going on in our apartment. A couple of minutes later, I came out of the door, lipstick bag in hand.

My mom said, "Oh Chandra, I wish you would've pledged. You would have been excellent. A girl with a heart for good—gosh, we missed a good one by not getting you."

"Yeah, but I would've been going through all the drama your daughter is facing."

"Say no more," my mom said, laughing. "Alright honey, we'll see you later."

"Yes ma'am."

Chandra motioned with her finger underneath her chin and lifted it toward the sky. I gave her a thumbs-up. I knew my newfound enemies were still my line sisters, and as I rode in the car with my mom, my stomach dropped with every mile.

"Sweetheart, you're turning blue over there," my mom said, looking at my light-skinned face as we arrived on campus, parked, and made our way to the ceremony at the theatre.

It wasn't that I was scared of Sharon, Dena, Bea and Audria, but I guess collectively all of them hating me wasn't something I was ready to walk into. Being in my apartment was what I wanted desperately.

"Come on girl, the Remembrance Ceremony is about to start," my mom said, as I lagged behind her.

When we got to the door, I cased the place over her shoulder, looking for my line sisters. I had no idea where I was going to sit. Certainly my mom was going to sit with her alumnae friends. However, she surprised me when she told the woman at the door that she needed two seats.

"Hey, is that your daughter? She's beautiful," the woman said to my mom, obviously knowing her.

"You don't remember me, do you?" she asked me. "I came to your house a few years back. I was on one of your mom's committees. I got the two little girls you helped babysit that night."

"Yeah, your baby's name is Rose. Every time I plaited her hair she pulled out all the barrettes and undid it."

"That's her," she laughed. "How ya doing?"

"She's not doing too great," my mom cut in, ready to tell all my business. "She's in this chapter here and girl, they got all kind of issues going on."

"I know."

"Mom!" I said, wanting to hit her.

"That's okay, she knows I understand. Sorority life can be extremely hard and stressful. After your mom served as committee chair, I took over the position, and the ladies on my committee started planning stuff without me, didn't show up to the things that I planned and asked me not to serve in that role anymore."

"Wow," I said, truly able to identify. "What did you do?"

"I prayed about it. Here I was, a grown woman in an alumnae chapter, trying to work toward change, and I had tears in my eyes over some petty foolishness, 'cause some lady on the committee didn't like the fact that I moved on if they didn't do what they said they were going to do. But after praying and really doing a lot of soul searching there was another committee the president needed me to chair. I started working with those ladies and everything has been fine. Sometimes it's personalities and insecurities from others you have to deal with."

"What happened with the ladies you used to be on the committee with?"

"We are actually fine now too. You can't run from the sisterhood. The good in those sorors—what made you love them in the first place—find that. They still have it in them, even if they lose their minds sometimes," she said, comforting me. "Here are some purple penlights for the ceremony," she said. "I hope everything works out for you."

I sat down with my mom and quickly spotted my crew across the room. They were giving me looks that could cut steel. This was so hard. I hated being estranged from those I cared for so much.

As water welled up in my eyes, my mom said, "Hold it together, girl. I would go talk to them myself, but I know that's not what you want."

"No, it's not."

"So hold it together. You will find a way to deal with all this. A leader is strong."

"I'm not their leader. I shouldn't have come."

"Shhh, the program is starting, and no one can take the leadership traits away from you."

The state director went to the mic and began the ceremony. "Every five years there's a new rotation started in remembrance of one of our five founders."

The lights dimmed and everyone turned on their purple pen lights.

"Miss Cleo Armstrong, from the great state of Virginia," the state director announced. "The first generation from her family to go to college. She never met a stranger and loved every soror. She was the first president of Beta Gamma Pi and when you told her you liked something, she ended up leaving it to you in her will."

Another soror said, "Soror Armstrong loved God. She loved her family, and she served this sorority. This entire year we will remember her by focusing on being the best leaders we can be. We might not make the best decisions, but as long as you lead from the soul everything will be okay."

When I looked over at my sorority sisters, a couple of them had tears in their eyes. I didn't know what all that was about, but the moment had certainly touched me as well. I wasn't a perfect president, but I certainly gave it all I had. I think Soror Armstrong is smiling at me from Heaven and that thought made me feel a bit of warmth in my cold situation.

It was now spring break and it felt great great to be heading with my roommates down to Gulfport, Mississippi, to relax on the beach and play a few slot machines. Our first priority was to spend time together to get reacquainted. All four of us had been going in such different directions we needed this time to reconnect again. After we checked into our luxurious hotel, we hit the beach.

As we lay there, all in our own worlds, thinking about whatever was on our minds, Chandra said, "You know what, guys, I just want to be honest."

"What, talk to us," Myra said.

"I guess I gave y'all a hard time about pledging your sororities and stuff because I felt like it pulled you away from what we had. We weren't first anymore, our sisterhood, our bond thing that made us the tightest freshmen around, is no more—and that is hard for me."

Bridget sat up and rubbed Chandra's back. "I'm sort of mad at my own sorority for making that happen. We used to have dinner at the house at least once a week and now that's sorority night for me, so I can't go."

Myra said, "Every time I want to do something, we're

either studying or planning some kind of event, so you're right, I allowed my sorority duties and ego to pull me away from our friendship too."

They looked at me, and I just had to keep it real and be honest with them. "It's not even like I'm all involved with my sorority anymore. After being kicked out, I guess I've been wallowing in my own self pity and I haven't opened up to you guys. But Bridget, I can't thank you enough for bringing Tammy and Penelope over to try and help. I don't think I ever thanked you properly. I guess what I'm saying is although it seems like we are going in different directions, we are still here for one another. Chandra, I don't think that will ever go away."

"But Chandra, you can pledge MEM and we can be even tighter," Bridget said.

"She knows she wants to wear brown and peach if she wears anything," Myra said.

"I can't even front and ask you to pledge Beta, we are so messed up," I said, as they laughed.

"I think I'm just fine being a G.D.I."

"What's that?" Bridget asked.

"Girl, you know that's a Got D . . . Independent," Chandra chimed out loudly.

"Oh, that's right," Bridget said, laughing.

"You know we love you right? And any time you want us to be better, just hit us in the head. You always been good at that," I teased.

"Hit *them* in the head," Bridget said. "You can just come and tell me."

"I hear y'all, thanks," Chandra said, feeling better as we shared a group hug.

Later on we played a few games in the casino. Myra and Chandra won fifty dollars apiece, but Bridget and I were losing money, so we decided to walk to the resort part of the hotel. I couldn't believe it when we came across two guys that were so fine neither one of us knew which one we wanted to talk to.

"Okay, they are gorgeous," I said.

"Chandra would approve, non-Greeks. If they were Greeks they would be sporting paraphernalia," Bridget said.

"Oh my gosh, they are coming this way," I told her.

One of the guys went over to Bridget and said something. The other one, who was a little taller and stockier, came over to me. All of my pearly whites were showing.

"I'm sorry, I know it must have seemed as if we were staring, but you two are gorgeous. Let me introduce myself. I'm Taylor Black, from Louisiana. The two of us should have dinner tonight."

"Well, I'm with my girls and I am sure they won't mind coming with us later tonight," I said, letting him know I wasn't going to be alone with him.

"Hey Hayden! I'll be right over here," Bridget said, as she walked with Taylor's friend around the corner.

"Looks like one of your girls is going to be occupied. You said you got two more. I got two friends too—maybe all eight of us could go to dinner."

"Yea, that works," I replied.

Later that evening, I was sipping on a glass of wine in Taylor's hotel room. I couldn't remember how I got there. Taylor's lips were going up and down my neck but

I was so confused. I could swear I was looking at Creed. I felt funny.

Trying to move away from him, I said, "Stop."

"What, you got a boyfriend or something?" Taylor asked, extremely irritated.

"I don't know you," I said boldly.

"Well, I'm trying to change that and make it a little bit better. Let my hands do some magic over your body. You'll get to know me just fine."

"We aren't even alone. Your friends are right in the other room," I said, as he slithered his hands up my shirt.

"And your friends are there too, so nothing can happen to you that you don't want to," he said, as he started feeling all over me.

"No!"

"I want to take this to the next level. Let me," he said, as he tried to unfasten my bra.

At that moment it was clear to me that I needed to find a way out of there. I don't know if it was the girls kicking me out of the sorority, or my breakup with Creed, but some way, some how, I was going to have to get a hold of my life and stop doing absolutely idiotic things. Yeah, this guy was fine, but I didn't know him. I was drinking with him, when I didn't even drink. What was I doing?

"Chandra, help me," I shouted out.

I moved to the corner of the bed. I was wobbly, but I needed him off me. I called out for Chandra again, this time louder and she quickly came into the room.

"You got to help me. I have to get out of here, I feel sick."

"Wait, don't take her anywhere, I got ya girl," Taylor said to Chandra.

"Naw partner, you don't know how deep our friendship is. Let's go, Hayden," she said.

She called out to Bridget and Myra. I felt so woozy. Then all three of them helped me out of Taylor's hotel room.

"Partner, she's just getting started. Bring her back," Taylor said, trying to convince my girls to leave me there.

Chandra snarled at him like a mama grizzly bear protecting her cub and said, "I am not your partner. Thanks for dinner. Maybe we'll see you guys around before we head back, but I'm going to take care of my girl. She's my priority."

BOLDLY

As soon as we got into our hotel room, Chandra threw me on the bed and hit me upside my head. "Okay, so do you think that was just the stupidest thing you ever did or what, girl?"

"What? What do you mean?" I said, groggy and disoriented.

"You don't drink and you had four glasses of wine. You don't even know that fool. He could've raped you!"

"I know, you're right. All I kept thinking about was Creed. When I realized this other guy's lips were all over me, I knew I was in over my head. Do you think Creed will forgive me?" I said, leaning my head on Chandra's lap.

"Girl, I'm going off on you right now, trying to make you understand that you have to become responsible and you talkin' about some other boy. Whatever, get this. You've got too much going on to be so careless," Chandra scolded.

"Well, the smartest thing she did was bring us with her," Myra said.

"You gotta admit though," Bridget interjected, "all those guys were cute!"

Chandra said, "Yeah, until they proved to be scum buckets."

"That's not-not-not nice to talk-talk about people," I said, slurring my words.

"You just hush," Chandra said to me, as she helped me get into bed.

"I'm feeling a little woozy too," Bridget said, leaning over.

Myra said, "See, I told you, Chandra! We saw those guys slip something into our drinks. I'm so glad we declined everything and we didn't leave with the two guys we were with."

"Yeah, we stood our ground and told them we weren't going nowhere," Chandra added.

"Thank you for not leaving me, thank you," I uttered, still feeling really bad. "You think they put something in our drinks? Oh my gosh, this is horrible. I'm gonna die!"

"Girl, you are not gonna die," Chandra said, taking off my shoes.

Finally, Bridget and I fell out.

The next morning, I had a headache. It felt like a ton of bricks was pressed up against my head.

"Come on, we got to get out of here. Let's go home," Chandra said. "Get up, you two!"

She tried getting me and Bridget up, but neither of us moved a muscle. I didn't have a lot of experience with being with guys that I didn't know. But obviously, I could see I'd made a mistake I didn't need to make again. How fortunate I was that my girls had my back.

"As soon as we got you home, you guys passed out! It's clear that those guys were up to no good for sure," Chandra said, reminding us of what transpired the night before.

Though I hated that I didn't have that kind of bond with my line sisters anymore, it was a serious blessing that I still had my roommates. We had all chosen different paths, but we still had a connection that showed up in the nick of time.

On the drive back home, Myra uttered, "So you know you were talking about Creed last night. I guess you haven't forgotten him, huh?"

"I hear he's still not dating anyone," Bridget uttered, throwing the hint that Tammy, her chapter president, had definitely left him alone.

"I was not talking about Creed. You guys are making that up," I said, knowing all the while that I truly did miss that man.

"Well, I know him," Chandra said, "and he'd be so mad that you threw yourself at the first guy that came along on a vacation."

"You got to admit, he was cute," Bridget said.

"Girl, will you quit that! You mentioned that last night. Cute's gonna get you killed," Chandra said.

Bridget swerved off the road and she joked, "Be nice to the driver. I can get you killed too. I'm behind the wheel."

"Girl, don't lose your mind," Chandra said to her.

The four of us laughed and joked all the way back home. Bridget and I still had splitting headaches, so we pulled over so Chandra could drive.

"Black women just don't like asking for help. We think we can do it all and be it all," Chandra said when she got behind the wheel. "I mean Bridget, you knew you were tired and weren't feeling well. Why didn't you just ask somebody else to drive?"

"I don't know," she said. "I'm just used to carrying a load."

"Yeah," Myra agreed. "It's very rare that other people pick up the slack for you or want to help, so you just have to learn how to deal with it and move on."

"Shouldn't our friendship be more?" I responded from the backseat. "Shouldn't we be bold enough to tell each other when we're not doing the right thing and strong enough to know that the criticism is coming for the right reasons?"

"Yes, so hear me," Chandra said. "You care about Creed and you care about those Beta girls. All you can do is let people know what's really going on in your heart. If they can't accept you after that, then don't worry about it. It's not on you. But you're not a coward and you're not perfect. So stand up and speak the truth. I think when you're really deep and true with the people you really care about, you'll be surprised at their reaction."

"Thanks," I said to her, and then I leaned back and prayed that all of my problems would just go away.

It was Pi Lambda Beta week and they were having an all-night outdoor slam filled with music, food and dancing. It must've been a night of new beginnings for me, because I stepped into the place wearing my Beta Gamma Pi letters. Even though I knew I was ostracized by my peers, those letters were still a part of me. Myra stood beside me with her Rho Tau Nu brown and peach T-shirt on and Bridget was on the other side sporting silver and gold. Chandra had some studying to do so she didn't make it.

Then of course a group of my line sisters walked in and cut between us, pushing me on my shoulder. It was rather rude. As soon as I could see who it was that pushed me, I was not shocked to see Bea.

But then a familiar voice said, "That was really rude."

When I looked over my other shoulder, I was surprised to see Trisha. I wanted to hug her, but I quickly remembered our relationship was strained. My feet didn't walk away, but I didn't move toward her either.

She smiled and said, "Hey Hayden. I haven't seen you in months. I hear you're on the outs like me. Not that you did anything to deserve it, but I'm sort of tired of being ostracized. I did wrong and I needed to come out of hiding, so here I am."

"We'll let you two talk," Myra said, pulling Bridget away.

"Do we have to leave?" Bridget said under her breath.

"I'll catch up with you two later," I laughed. I had such great friends, ready to give me privacy to work out my differences with my soror.

"You hate me, don't you?" Trisha said boldly when I didn't return her smile.

"No, I don't hate you. You probably hate me for exposing it all. I had to be the one to try to do what's right, and I think I just ended up pushing everyone away."

"No, you were right to call me out, even though it hurt. I think it's made me better. I've cheated on tests in school. I've stolen a pair of jeans from the mall. I've even told the bank that I deposited more money than I really had, and convinced them their system was wrong," Trisha confessed. Her news shocked me. "I don't know, I've always been just trying to get it worked out. It's just hard. Not having money to go to school messed me up in some other areas. Breaking the law is never good. You pushed for me to be treasurer when we were voting that day. You believed that I would have your back and do what was right and I didn't. I let you down."

"It's alright, girl. We all mess up," I said, remembering I needed grace myself and giving her a big hug.

"Do you mean it? Hayden, really? You forgive me?"

"Girl, I am not God and I'm certainly no jury."

She said, "Thanks for convincing the girls to help me raise the money I needed to pay the sorority back. I won't have to go to jail. I can't even tell you how much I owe you. What can I do?"

"Just be you," I said to her, really happy that though the chapter hated helping her, we did something good for Trisha.

"You sure you want me to do that?" she said, reflecting on her past.

"Okay, well be a better you than you have ever been before. But you can't get away from who you are, Trisha. You can't run away from things that tempt you. You have got to fix you from the inside, or when no one's looking you'll mess up again."

"I hear what you're saying," she said, as she started

smiling. "Well, hey, it looks like somebody wants to talk to you. We'll chat later."

"Huh?" I said, confused.

Then she pointed behind me. When I turned, my eyes got so wide. It was Creed.

"I was hoping you'd come out tonight," he said, cutting straight to the chase. "I miss you, girl."

Then all of a sudden, Butch appeared on my right and Butch started yanking on my arm. "Hey, wait a minute! We ain't gonna have none of that here. I told you, man. I'm trying to get with her."

"Ow!" I yelled, as I felt him squeeze me.

"Man, let her go."

"You ain't gonna tell me what to do!" Butch said, pushing Creed back.

"*You* ain't gonna tell *me* what to do. Let her go!" Creed shouted.

"Please let my hand go, ow!" I said, yanking it away.

Of course Myra and Bridget came over to my side quickly. Everybody piled around Creed and the jerk.

"I know you my frat brother, boy, but I'm tired of you pushing me around. You ain't even gotta haze me no more, I already got my letters," Creed hollered out.

"You will do whatever I say, when I say it." He came over and pushed Creed again.

"You better get Creed out of here," Myra said to me. "He needs to be away from that crazy fool."

"Come on, Creed, let's go. He ain't even worth it," I said, as I tugged at Creed's arm.

"I got this, Hayden, please! I'm sick and tired of his big mouth. Always trying to get up in my face."

"Oh, you gonna let your woman try to come and tell you to get away from the fire. Wimp," Butch said.

"That's just the point. Now, you get it. She ain't yours," Creed said to him.

"Whatever, man."

"Come on, Creed, let it go. Let him call us whatever names he wants. Let's go." Creed finally walked with me away from Butch.

Butch yelled, "I don't want her stuck-up, virgin tail no way. She ain't gonna want you after she know all the honeys you been hittin' since you got your letters."

Automatically, my heart sank to the ground. If Creed wanted to stand there and argue with him, that was his choice. I could no longer deal with it. I knew Creed and I weren't together, but a part of my heart belonged to him and it hurt to hear he had been with other girls. Before we could be reunited, clearly we were through, 'cause his heart did not belong to me.

"Hayden, wait up, wait up! Come on now, please, wait up!" Creed said to me as I walked to my car. "Come on now. Give me a chance to explain."

"What? What do you have to say to me? Was Butch lying?"

I got no answer. I threw my hands in the air—his silence was proof he was a dog. "Okay then. Just let me go."

Bridget's voice was behind me. "Wait up, Hayden. Here we come."

Then I heard Myra tell Creed, "Please, just let her go.

She's been through a lot. She can't deal with this right now."

"And to think I told her you weren't messing with nobody," Bridget said in a nasty way, which was so the opposite of my friend.

Those two were being so sweet. I loved their support of me dearly. I so learned that being there for your friend through anything was what every friend should try and do.

"Nah, y'all, I need to talk to her," I heard Creed say. "I need to talk to her now."

I just kept walking. Creed needed to go back to the party and walk on up to another girl. Yes, he was fine, smart, and now a Pi, but so what.

He ran up to me all out of breath and said, "Please, please give me a chance to explain."

"You just stood in my face and told me that you miss me, but you forgot to tell me the part that you have been with other girls. Is that true?"

"It's not true."

"What's not true?"

"Okay, okay. I was with this one girl, but I was drunk. I was thinking about you and it was a mess."

All of a sudden, he spoke to my core. I knew what it was like not to be perfect. I had just come back from spring break and I come close to doing the exact same thing. Because I didn't go all the way, did that mean I was better than him?

"I'll talk to him, y'all," I said to Bridget and Myra as they stood by, always having my back.

"I'll bring her home," he told them.

"You cool with that?" Myra asked.

"Well, she knows him. It's not like he's gonna slip something in her drink like the other guy," Bridget said, then she covered her lips as her eyes widened at what she'd let slip.

"Girl, hush!" Myra said.

"What do you mean, somebody slipped something in your drink? It wasn't . . ." He didn't even finish before he turned, ready to go back to the house.

"No! It wasn't Butch," I said, holding him back before he went in to have the fight he had just walked away from. "I got this, y'all. I'm cool. He'll bring me home."

We drove around town, not stopping at any particular destination. I didn't want him over to my house. I didn't want to go to his. We were together, but we weren't even speaking to one another. Could our relationship even be fixed? Could we find our way back to each other? Could we have a relationship that was worth something? I think both of us were pondering those thoughts.

"You hungry?" Creed asked, finally breaking the silence.

"Yeah," I said, knowing we had left the Pi slam before the ribs and chicken got on the grill.

"Yeah, I could have a little bite to eat. I remember when I took you to that restaurant on the other side of town. You were diggin' the Philly cheesesteak sandwich. Want another one of those?"

"Yeah, that'd be great," I told him.

When we got to the restaurant, as soon as we were seated, Creed said, "I'm sorry."

"For what?" I asked him.

"Letting you down. Carrying on with some other girl I didn't even like just to satisfy myself. I came away feeling emptier than before I even messed with her. I'm just a typical frat guy now, hit 'em and leave 'em."

"Maybe that's why I like you. Because I know you care more than that."

Creed asked, "You think the letters got to the both of us? Pulled us too far apart?"

"I was such a horrible leader in my sorority."

"Yeah, I wasn't too great in our relationship either," he said.

"What do you mean?"

"Well, I got a little jealous that you were all excited about Beta Gamma Pi. So when my frat called me, I was the first one there. I tried to spend time with you, but there were times when you were busy and it just seemed like it happened all the time when I wanted to hang out with you. I tried to voice my opinion but I didn't know if you were really hearing me."

"Wow," I said.

"Yeah, wow. I'm admitting this to you because I was wrong. I should have worked with you to help you find a balance. Call you out in a way that made sense so you could understand what I needed. I know you care about me."

"I do," I said to him. "I was with that guy on spring break, just frustrated and mad because I didn't have you."

"I don't want to scare you, Hayden, but I do want us to try again."

"Why would that scare me?"

"Because when a man can't stop thinking about a woman, when he's with somebody else and he's still thinking about that woman, you know he loves that lady."

"What?" I said.

"I love you," he said boldly.

17

GLORY

It felt like I was hearing the Heavenly angels sing when Creed said he loved me. I jumped up from the table so quickly and leapt into his arms. I had been fighting my feelings for him, but now I knew from the very core that he owned my heart. It wasn't just that he was handsome or that he was Greek, he truly was there for me, like my housemates. He wasn't putting up with any of my stuff, but he was kind even when I drove him away. I knew I shouldn't have neglected him—a mistake that I hoped I would never make again. With ketchup on my lip from the Philly cheesesteak sandwich, I kissed him and the few people in the restaurant applauded.

"You've never been one to show emotion in public, now look at you," he said.

"You said you loved me. The thing is, I love you too." Then he kissed me again.

Whistles and cheers came from our audience at that

point. For the next hour, he and I sat and talked about all the things we had wanted to tell each other while we were apart.

As we rode home, I looked out of the window. I was so very thankful to have another chance with Creed, but there was still a hole burning my soul.

Tuning in to my feelings, he stroked the side of my cheek and said, "You want to get things right with the Betas, huh?"

I just smiled. No need to say it. I mean it was obvious, but how? I thought time would mend things, instead it just made them worse. I didn't even know who the Betas had decided to make president. My mom had even encouraged me to talk to them, but I just couldn't face them. Besides, the little shove I received at the party showed they obviously weren't thinking kindly about me. Yeah, in my mind, I knew the damage was too far gone to be reversed. Though technically I was a part of them, in my heart I didn't feel like I was at all. I looked back out of the window. I couldn't even face Creed to answer his question.

"Talk to me," my guy said, truly into me.

"It's just not going to work out for me to be a Beta anymore, Creed. And if you want a girlfriend who is Greek, then maybe I am not the girl for you."

"Wait now, don't even play me like that," he said. "If you're not active with them that's not going to make me not want to be with you. Give me more credit than that. I just told you I loved you. I've never said those words to a girl *ever*—my feelings for you are deep. They are also real. I'm not saying I deserve any praise. I'm just saying, give me the benefit of the doubt."

"I'm sorry," I said. All he was trying to do was be someone I could talk to and work off of. But once again, I put my foot in my mouth. "I guess only God can help me work all of this out."

"Well, have you talked to Him? Have you prayed about it?"

"That's interesting—I can't even remember the last time I prayed. I've just been going through the motions. That's how I ended up with some guy I didn't know, wishing I was with you and . . . you don't want to hear all of that," I said, realizing I was talking too much.

"RIGHT! I don't want to hear all of that. I wish I would have known that you wanted to work things out with me. My spring break was miserable, Hayden, because I didn't know where you were. Maybe your girls are miserable without you around them too."

"They haven't called."

"I haven't called you either. Sometimes people are afraid of rejection. They kicked you out, what do they look like coming back asking for forgiveness and for you to come back. I'm sorry, but I know them."

"Well, I saw a couple of them tonight at your party. One of them brushed by me and never said excuse me. It was like an intentional jab. There's nothing that can be fixed between us."

"Well, like you said, maybe nothing you can fix on your own. But if you believe in the One up above in Heaven and you know He granted your desire by allowing you to be a member of the organization in the first place, then He can show you how to resolve this with His word. I don't know many scriptures, but I certainly know about the one where it goes, 'Come to me all ye who are weary and heavy laden.' "

"Yeah," I said, " 'And I will give you rest . . . Place your cares upon me because my yoke is easy and my burden is light.' "

"See, you feel it. You can even quote it," Creed said to me. "Stand on it, Hayden."

We were at my door. I hugged him tight and said, "Thanks Lord, for giving me this guy. Let us do it your way. Amen. Now Creed, get out of here. I'm fine."

"No, I'm just going to wait until you get inside."

"I'm fine. I see you giving me a hard time," I said.

Before I could get upstairs to the dimly lit front door of my apartment, Butch, my ex-boyfriend, came from the bushes and grabbed me, putting his hand over my mouth. Even though I tried to yell as loud as I could, his big rough hands prevented anything from coming out.

"I was wondering when you were going to come home. I thought you were going to stay out all night. You wouldn't give it up to me last year, but you gonna be all into the boy I made a Pi? How you think that makes me look? Answer me. Answer me!" he yelled out as he shook me hard.

I couldn't answer him. He was still holding on to me as he dragged me back behind the bushes. I knew he was a jerk, which is why I broke up with him. But I didn't know he could be so over-the-top and violent. He had already hurt my arm earlier in the evening. What in the world was he planning to do to me now? And Creed had wanted to wait when he dropped me off, but dumb me told him to go on. I was only ten feet away from my door. Now, I was scared.

"I'm a senior, about to graduate. I got a job waiting on me. I'm going to be a lawyer one day and you trying to tell me that you don't want this."

"HELP!" I yelled out, but a mean sucker punch caught me in my jaw. The gory taste of my own blood filled my mouth.

"I'm sorry. I didn't meant to do that," he said, getting real close to me.

His sweet attitude change reminded me of Dr. Jekyll and Mr. Hyde. I could smell the alcohol on his breath.

"You can't deny what is mine. Don't cause no trouble. We'll have a good little party. Then I'll let you go on your merry little way. After I get mine, I won't care if Creed takes my leftovers. Now though, I want this and I know you ain't gave it to him yet," Butch said, as he put his hand up my shirt.

My eyes watered as he unbuckled his pants while one arm was around my throat. "Don't do this."

"I didn't want our first time to be like this. I didn't want it to be outside. I wanted it to be comfortable on a nice plush bed. You know I got a waterbed at my apartment, but you wouldn't work with me. You wouldn't give me what I deserved, so now I've just got to take it. Don't fight me though. You'll love it."

He was having trouble getting his pants all of the way

down and when he eased up off of me just a little, I used my elbows to move backward. Nothing was going in my favor. I could not get away.

Angrily he snarled, "I tried to play it right last year, Hayden. I took you to all those fancy little dinners, introduced you to all of the right people and you basically spat in my face by breaking up with me. We're not in high school anymore so of course I'm going to want a little piece. But I was willing to let that go. I could have made up some rumor about you to save my reputation, but then you got to parade one of my frat brothers all up in my face. He gonna try to stand up for you at a party because I want what's mine. Whatever, I'ma show him. He couldn't get you to give him none. At the end of the day he is the weaker man. You try to play that little innocent role, but deep within I know you're easy."

My body temperature was rising so fast. I disliked Butch before this, but now I hated him. I mustered up as much spit and blood as I could and spat it right in his face.

"You hussy! But that's good—don't play the victim, give me a little of that sauce. I know you've got some within you, make it fun for me. Fight me, fight me!" he said as he ripped open my shirt and put his filthy hands all over my chest.

"Stop it, stop it! Get off of me!" I screamed.

"What, I didn't do enough to get you to shut up? What, you trying to get me in trouble? You trying to get people to come out here?"

Lord, You've got to help me. I know I haven't talked to You in a while and I know it always seems that I come and talk to You when I am at my lowest, but this guy is going to really hurt me, I prayed.

Then I heard my front door open and the light come on. "Hayden, are you out there?" Chandra called.

"Y'all, we've got to find her," Bridget said.

"She's out here somewhere," Myra said.

He quickly covered my mouth. I knew as he looked around, he was panicked. Rightfully so. He cornered me when I was helpless. How cowardly.

"Dang it!" Butch said.

It didn't matter from that point that he was frustrated. So was I. I was already beat up. He had taken a lot from me, but he wasn't going to take what he wanted. With my free hand, I pinched between his legs and when he jerked up, I yelled, but I wasn't loud enough.

"Where is she?" Creed asked in a panic. "I dropped her off. I'm so glad one of you guys answered your house phone."

"Her car is here, but she's not inside. I'm calling the cops," Bridget said, running back into the house.

"Help!" I screamed again, louder this time. Butch hit me again.

The next thing I knew, Creed was pounding Butch's face. My girls helped me off the cold, hard ground and took me inside.

Hallelujah, I thought, as I saw tears of joy flow from their eyes. I must have looked horrible. God heard my plea and looked out for me. *Hallelujah*, I thought as tears came from my eyes as well, as I knew what the Lord had just allowed me to escape from.

* * *

After giving a statement to the police, I was able to relax some. Turns out Creed had only gone a few miles up the road before he called my house to see if I had made it in. Chandra told him I wasn't in the house, so he immediately turned around and they came out looking for me.

When I looked into the mirror, I didn't even recognize myself. After initially refusing, I ended up going to the emergency room for treatment. Word spread around campus pretty fast. Though they were keeping me overnight for observation, I was surprised to wake up and see Bea, Audria, Dena and Sharon standing over me.

"She's waking up, y'all," Sharon said.

I tried to say hello, but my jaw and mouth were too swollen. I wanted to tell them I was sorry and to please give me another chance. But I guess the tears that welled up in my eyes told them all they needed to hear.

"We're sorry too," Audria said.

"Especially me," Bea said, as she came onto the other side of the bed and held my hand. "Am I hurting you? Hayden, I pushed you away. Now I just want you to go off on me, because I guess hearing you fuss at me would be better than having you say nothing at all. I was so wrong."

"I told these jokers to call you a long time ago," Dena said.

"Well, you know that we couldn't make up our mind as to who would be president, so you're still it. So you've got to come back to us."

"Yeah," Audria said, "I've been praying that we all get together. I've been feeling bad because I asked the Lord to make it happen at any cost. We need you. However, I didn't want you to end up in the hospital."

"If I see Butch myself I could just kill him," Bea said, with an angry look I had never before seen. And I had seen Bea angry.

She'll have to get in line on that one, I thought, as I tried to crack a smile. It was so good to see them all.

"I know you've got a lot of people that care for you. It's amazing to me that a GDI, MEM, a Nu and a Beta could all get along like you and your roommates have proven to do this year. I think deep down, a couple of us were jealous of that relationship. We're supposed to be sisters and have that emotional bond, but we failed you."

"Yeah," Dena said, "we failed you while you were trying to encourage us to be the best that we could be. So when Bridget called and told us you were in here we had to come."

Bea said, "And when Trisha did wrong, you didn't give up on her. Because we were able, you had us lend a hand and we resented you for that."

"And even at Founders' Day, we were moved," Sharon said. "We should have come to you then to try and work it all out. I saw you all over there, emotional, just as your eyes are now, and you care deeply for us even with all of our faults. And you've got a guy that cares about you— Creed is the man. You've got roommates that care. But they're not the only ones, which is what I guess I am trying to say."

"Yeah, as pitiful as we are," Bea said, "we love you too. We need you back leading us, showing us the way."

"And to show you we are really sincere," Dena said.

"It wasn't just because of all of this that happened tonight, even though I am glad we found out, because we brought you lilies."

That was so sweet. It was the sorority flower and they brought them to me. When you give them to a soror it shows your deep love and care for her.

"I wasn't trying to be a dictator," I uttered slowly, trying not to irritate my cut jaw.

"Shhh, don't talk. I know," Sharon said. "You just had stubborn folks trying to do the job we elected you to."

"Tell her, Dena. Tell her what you were saying."

"Yeah!" Dena said, "I told them the convention was coming next month and they don't have anyone running for National Second Vice President. We think you should run."

"Well, I'll help with your campaign," Sharon said. "You're a person who truly wants the best for our sorority. You stepped away from it yourself just to please us. You gave us time and space and I think because of it we were able to see how wrong we were."

"I'm still sorry," I said, in a voice that I didn't recognize. "I didn't want to push y'all away."

"We understand that," Bea said. "But will you forgive us? Do you still love us? Will you still be our president?"

"Yes," I nodded.

Audria said, "Well, you ain't Jesus, but right now, I say, thank you Lord. We are in a mess. We need you back. We need to nurse you back to health and get you out of this hospital because you're the only one that can get us back on the right track."

"I don't deserve all of that. You guys can do it though."

Sharon took my hand and rubbed it. "What happened to you tonight was awful. We are so sorry. These kinds of things you don't deserve. You're an awesome person, Hayden, and you need to hear that sometimes. You deserve praise and glory."

PLATINUM

"What the hell do you want, Hayden?" Keisha yelled into the phone as I pulled it away from my ear for a second so I wouldn't hear her harsh word. "Hayden, did you hear me? What do you want?"

"Look, you don't have to cuss at me," I said to the ring leader who had caused most of the drama when I was on line.

"I don't have time to hold your hand and be all sweet and nice. Because of you wimps I'm out of the sorority, okay. Why are you calling me?"

She had me there for a second. I just had to pause. So much had gone on this whole year. It was now the beginning of May and though a month had passed since Butch's brutal attack, I was still a little shaken. Thankfully he was behind bars. After my chapter came to me and asked me to lead them again, we spent several weeks on public service: giving to the community, giving to kids, doing deep study sessions to make sure we all aced our exams, and even with all that, there was still a part of our chapter that needed to heal.

I didn't know if our chapter could be completely healed with half of the members either suspended or about to graduate. But certainly before they walked out of Western Smith we could share and begin the healing process. Edythe, Penelope, and several other members were all on board. Keisha was the one person that we most wanted to talk to. Even some of her own line sisters hadn't talked to her since they had been sentenced to stay away.

Knowing that I couldn't back down I said, "I'm calling because I want you to be a part of our meeting."

"Girl, I heard about your little meeting. My line sisters called me—they hadn't called me in months. But now they talking 'bout we need to sit before you guys and answer questions," Keisha said angrily, then paused. "Please, whatever. Don't look for me to show up. I won't be there."

"Can you tell me why?" I said. "Why are you so opposed to it? I am going to make sure it is not a bashing session."

"I don't even care if it's going to be a stone-throwing session. I can take all of y'all's little comments. Regardless of what people tell me I am supposed to do, I have my own view. Because y'all didn't go through everything we had planned, I still think you are nothing but paper."

"You're entitled to your opinion, Keisha," I said, not wanting to argue with her. "And if there are some things you want to say to everybody, now would be a perfect time to . . ."

"What for? Why would putting all those feelings out on the table help?"

"Because if you keep them bottled up inside, how can everyone move on? This is about all of us healing."

"Well I'm moving on. I'm transferring from here next year. I'm not coming back, so you can do whatever you want to do and say whatever you want to say about me. If I had to do this all over again, I might have believed that the girl was allergic to peanuts but other than that I would have not made it any easier on you guys. So what you got to say to that?"

"I know that I can't make everything perfect, Keisha. I'm actually sorry I haven't talked to you until this point," I said sincerely. "But honestly, I didn't know what to say. You say we are paper. You say we are unworthy to be Betas. To keep it real, we made a lot of mistakes without you prophytes around. You called us out on one of those mistakes the day we weren't protecting our spot on the yard."

"Yep, and if I still would have been a Beta I would have been able to teach you guys those things. But y'all know so much."

Glad she was letting me in on her thoughts, I said, "You believe right to be one thing and I truly believe right is something else. You are still my sister, and just like my birth sister gets on my nerves a lot of the time, I still love her."

"Oh, so you trying to tell me you love me? You ain't never called me all semester, but you love me?"

"Maybe the right answer is I am connected to you in a way that I cannot even explain. The feelings I have for you are automatic. I don't think hazing somebody and demeaning them makes you closer because if you believe that, then why do you say you are not connected to us? So what purpose did hazing us serve in the end? I don't like that you're transferring. I hate that none of this worked out, but I guess I just wanted you to know that at least I can say I am here for you, if you ever want to talk."

"Whatever Hayden, bye."

When I placed the phone down, I just felt real disappointed. The ultimate goal for a leader is to make everyone happy and get the job done. It was evident that I wasn't going to be able to do that.

When I got to the meeting later that day I shared Keisha's perspective with the old sorors and my line sisters.

Edythe, the former president, stood up and said, "Hayden, you did what you could. You shared your heart, and a lot of us have not done that with her yet. That is what the sisterhood is about. That's what being the right leader is about, going to your sister when she is down. Anybody can be close when things are perfect, when everybody is in accord, but it's a lot harder when everyone is in disagreement—then there's always going to be drama. But I think having all of us here to avoid some of that is the first step in getting the Alpha chapter sisterhood back on track, and honestly we have you to thank for that. You can't please everybody, and sometimes the people at the root of the problem don't want to change, so they need to go."

Penelope said, "Keisha was my line sister and because I followed her I can't even be a part of you guys anymore. You care about what she thinks more than I do. Relax girl, you are doing a good job. That's why we are about to move on from all this and talk about you winning National Second Vice President in a couple of weeks."

"Yeah!" they all cheered.

This sisterhood could be special if you just gave it your all.

The National Convention was held every year. This year it was in Washington, D.C. The Little Rock chapter, Creed and some of his frat brothers, my line sisters, and my roommates were all attending. College students and other Greek organizations attended convention because it's a great way to meet other Greeks and have fun. But they were on deck as part of my campaign crew to help me have a splash from the floor. Everybody had their ears and eyes open, with people in the other four regions trying to see if someone else was going to run from another chapter. We hadn't heard of anybody, so honestly I wasn't really that worried because I thought I would be unopposed.

However, when the call for nominations came, before someone from my chapter could nominate me, someone from the host chapter stood and nominated their chapter president. When that girl stood and addressed the mic, I slid down in my chair. You would have thought that she had on the Queen of England's jewels and I had on fake ones from a swap meet. She just seemed so poised, so together and I just felt out of my league.

"Beta Gamma Pi Sorority," the nominee said, "deserves the finest kind of representation. I am not someone who just became a Beta yesterday. I pledged two years ago. I have a four-point GPA and even with a full plate, I am ready to serve you. Elect me—Salina Dee—Second V.P."

After they nominated me, I had to address the five hundred delegates representing three hundred alumnae chapters and two hundred collegiate ones. I hadn't really prepared a speech because I thought it was just going to be me up there. Mental note to myself: *You never rise to the occasion, you only default to your level of training.* I should've prepared. I should have come up with something, but all I had was why I truly wanted the position.

So I got up and said, "It was only nine months ago when I was inducted into this illustrious sorority. It was the happiest day of my life. The dream I wanted for so long came true for me. Due to unforeseen circumstances, I not only ended up leading my line, but I also ended up being elected Chapter President. Looking back on those past months there were so many things I did right. I read all the manuals, I followed protocol, I held my meetings regularly and I cared deeply about what happened to every member of my chapter. But even with all that, I still got hurt. And there were so many times that I wanted to say, 'you know what, to heck with Beta Gamma Pi.' "

At that point, I could hear sorors mumbling and whispering. Though I was making up the speech as I talked, every word I said was coming from my heart. No pretense, only realness.

I continued, "But deep down I knew I couldn't walk away because I'd hurt some people in my chapter. I felt guilty, but above all, I thought I wasn't doing the sorority any good. So I said, forget Beta Gamma Pi. But what kept me going on is knowing none of us is perfect. As your Second Vice President there is no way I could stand before you now, asking you to elect me because I will be a perfect leader. But I can ask you to elect me because I have a heart to serve and I will strive daily not to let you down. As I balance my academics and my social life, Beta Gamma Pi will be a priority in my life. I want to make sure every collegiate follows the high standards that our founders call us all to adhere to. This is something I would dedicate my tenure to in this position, if so elected. Yes, we have young voices, but we are collegiates who love Beta Gamma Pi, and as your Second Vice President, not only am I willing to serve, but I won't stop serving until each task is done."

I received a standing ovation from my campaign crew. After that, my mom was busy planning, and my line sisters were busy campaigning. Talks were going on behind the scenes with the voting delegates, but then came the slander from the other candidate. It got leaked that under my watch as president my treasurer stole money. When the time for voting came, I lost by an overwhelming number. Though everyone who helped me consoled me, I felt horrible that the gold chain of trust and sisterhood was broken beyond repair. Basically, nobody wanted me and that hurt.

"Hayden, it's for you. It's the National President," Bea said to me as she held the hotel phone in her shaking hand.

"Okay, I know you're trying to cheer me up and all, but come on. Who's playing the joke here? I don't feel like talking. Tell whatever soror is on the phone that I'm alright."

"Take the call, Hayden," my mom said, as she rubbed my back.

I just wanted everybody to leave me alone. Why my mom wanted me to take some crazy call from one of my line sisters was beyond me.

"Mom, I'm tired. I just want to go to sleep. I don't need anybody to feel sorry for me."

"Hayden, it is the National President. She talked to me earlier. Take the phone now," my mom demanded.

"I think it's her for real," Bea said. "Your mom is right, take the phone."

Clearing my throat, I took the phone. "Hello," I said in a skeptical tone.

"Hayden Grant, hello, this is your National President speaking. I must tell you I am very impressed with you, young lady. You were poised and sharp and definitely have a heart for our sorority."

"Thank you," I said. "I know you're very busy, you didn't have to call. I'm okay."

"Oh dear, I am sure you are alright. Not only are you a leader, but I can tell you are determined and you're a fighter. Because of your tenaciousness, there is something I would like to talk to you about. I have a few minutes before I get ready for the closing assembly. Can you come up to my room now so we can have a chat?"

"Yeah, yes ma'am," I said, feeling all giddy inside. "What's your room number?"

Then I heard her giggle slightly. "I'm in the presidential suite on the top floor."

"Oh, I'm sorry," I said, feeling like such a novice.

"No, I love your energy. You know talking to my collegiates always keeps me humble. I'll see you in a second."

"Yes ma'am, I'll be right up."

Bea and Sharon started screaming. I was so excited to see them all excited. My mom also smiled.

"She just wants to talk to me. I don't know what it is all about. She probably just wants to look at me and see for herself if I am okay."

"I think she has more than that to ask you," Bea said.

Sharon said, "She's calling your phone and wants you to come up there. Maybe she found out what the other girl did and they ousted her and they are going to appoint you tonight."

"Now, now, let's not get ahead of ourselves. Let's leave all the dirty politics alone," my mom said. "What's for Hayden is for her.

"I've got to go get dressed myself. Hayden, I'll walk you out to the elevator. I am very proud of how you girls pulled together and really formed a unique sisterhood. You might have lost a big election now, but that pales in comparison to the great comradery you gained. You're winners. See you girls tonight."

"Thanks," Bea said.

"Yeah, we really appreciate that, Mrs. Grant," Sharon said.

My mom and I stepped into the hallway. She gave me a big hug. I truly felt her love.

"You know I am proud of you. I remember when you first started the school year I was so sad you were growing up. All you talked about was Beta Gamma Pi this and

Beta Gamma Pi that. Shucks, I just wanted to make sure you stayed a virgin. Tell me you're still a virgin."

"Mom, I'm still a virgin."

"Well, I am so glad that Butch guy didn't take what the Lord intends to be special."

I laid my head on her shoulder, completely agreeing with her. "Is it okay that I am going to go see this lady that beat you in a regional election years back?"

"Yeah, she's our National President and she's been doing a great job. I think she's grown a lot since that election, and if she offers you anything on her cabinet you consider taking it. You've got a lot to offer, my sweet lady. If she just wants to give you a few kind words, then you graciously take that too."

"Okay, Mom," I said, as I stepped into the elevator and she turned back to our room. "I love you."

She smiled back and said, "I love you too, baby."

Moments later I was at the door of the presidential suite. "So Miss Grant, come in. I won't keep you long. I have to get ready. I just want to let you know that elections can be brutal sometimes. I'm sure your mother schooled you on the one she and I were in years back. Though I'm not completely proud of my actions in that campaign, I think the difficulties of the job have humbled me time and time again. So here I stand. There are two reasons why I wanted to see you. First, I have a daughter who is a freshman at Western Smith."

"Wow, I didn't know that," I said.

"Yes, she made it her plan in life not to become a Beta and I am pretty familiar with everything that is going on with your chapter. But now that I've had a chance to speak to you, I am very pleased your leadership abilities. I know you are really able to recruit the types of women we need in our Alpha chapter. Need I say more?"

I got it. She called me up here because she wanted to make sure her daughter was on the next line, and the girl didn't even want to pledge. How was I going to make that happen? I couldn't say no to the National President.

Firmly, I said, "Yes ma'am. I understand."

"Well great. Because you are such a dynamic leader and we are able to have these sisterly talks, I want you to know I'm creating a new position on my cabinet. I want you to be chair of Collegiate Affairs. I want this committee to work to be a bridge between the young sorors and the alumnae sorors. A lot of the other organizations have some type of alumnae outreach program and it's really worked. Since we have a severe drop-out rate after sorors graduate college, I want to make sure great young women like you don't get lost. There's no pressure, you don't have to answer now."

"Well, I can't say no to my National President. Whenever you call on me to serve, I am here and ready."

"Being involved with Nationals is never easy, but it can be the most rewarding. Do you think being a Beta has made you better?"

"That is such a good question. I've learned how to be an effective me. Might not be the brightest, might not be the coolest, but I've got to work with what I've got, and when I maximize that, I'm much better from being in the organization."

She gave me a look of pride I'd never forget and then

she said, "I wish all of our college sorors could have your spirit."

As I left her room, I felt like a new artist whose album just went gold. Things were finally better than I'd ever dreamed. I had a great guy who loved me, best friends who'd do anything for me, line sisters who appreciated my tough leadership, and parents who knew they'd raised a daughter who made them proud. Come to think about it, now that the National President asked me to work with her in my beloved sorority, I felt like I was more than gold, I was double platinum.

Beta Gamma Pi, Book 1:

Work What You Got

Stephanie Perry Moore

ABOUT THIS GUIDE

The following questions are intended to
enhance your group's reading of
Beta Gamma Pi: WORK WHAT YOU GOT
by Stephanie Perry Moore

DISCUSSION QUESTIONS

1. Hayden Grant wants to pledge a sorority at any cost. Do you think her mother is giving her wise advice at the beginning of the book? What do you think is the correct pledge process?

2. Hayden finds out that her roommates all decide not to pledge Beta Gamma Pi with her, but decides to pledge anyway. What do you do when your friends change their mind and you feel like you've been left hanging? What are ways to boost your confidence so you can move on?

3. Though Hayden knows it is wrong, she participates in underground hazing. Why do we feel the need to give in to pressure to be accepted? What are ways to stand up for what is right and not go along to get along?

4. Most of the girls on the underground line end up not making the actual pledge line. Do you think a person can make a line if they do not participate in underground activities? What lesson is learned from taking that type of risk?

5. On the pledge line, all of the girls participate in some form of hazing activity. When things turned violent should this have been reported? What are better ways to unite a group?

6. When Hayden is voted line president, she feels overwhelmed. Do you think she was the best choice for this position? What qualities do you possess to be a great leader?

7. Hayden's boyfriend Creed is also pledging. How does what he's going through help Hayden? What are ways you can lean on a friend to help you through tough situations?

8. The big sisters of Beta Gamma Pi are suspended from the chapter for hazing. Hayden knows that her friend Penelope is upset about being kicked out of the sorority and offers comforting words. How can you help lift a person up when their actions have them feeling down? Do you agree with the comforting words Hayden gives to her friend Penelope about being kicked out of the sorority?

9. Hayden is now voted Chapter President. What do you think of how she led the group? How can being a good follower make a great leader?

10. Hayden has a called meeting and apologizes for her harsh tactics. Do you think it is okay to be vulnerable as a leader? What are ways to keep the Lord in your heart as you help to lead His way?

Stay tuned for the next book in the series,
THE WAY WE ROLL,
available in May 2009, wherever books are sold.
Until then, satisfy your Beta Gamma Pi craving with
the following excerpt from the next installment.

ENJOY!

BECOMING

If I see one more Beta Gamma Pi girl looking down at me because I am not sporting any of them pitiful letters, I might just kick her tail. Yes, I am here at their convention but I am not Greek. I'm not here like other wannabes, I'm here because I have to be.

My mom is their National President and that makes me sick. I hate that my time with my mom has taken a backseat to the sorority. For real, when it came to my mom doing sorority business over being a mom, I came last every time. Yeah, she said it was for the good of the community and one day I'd understand her sacrifice, but when she didn't make any of my piano recitals or parent-teacher conferences, I quickly learned to detest the group she dearly loved.

Though we lived in the same house—my dad and younger brother moved out after the divorce—my mom and I were worlds apart. Basically, I felt Beta Gamma Pi took everything away from me. I was only at the National Convention because some of the ladies on the executive board were more like mothers to me than my own mom. The First Vice President, who lived in California, begged me to come and support their endeavors. Because she was always there when I needed someone to talk to, I came. And not to mention the V.I.P. rooms were stocked with alcohol—and with no one around to supervise, I was feeling really nice.

"You're all smiles. I guess you just finished kissing the National President's butt, huh?" I said to a girl coming out of my mom's presidential suite.

"I'm sorry, do I know you?" the girl said, trying to figure out who I was.

"You're so full of it," I said, calling her out as I fumbled with my key, trying to open my hotel room door. "You know who I am, trying to get on my good side to raise your stock with her."

The girl persisted. "I'm sorry, I'm not trying to offend you, but you really do look familiar. Do you need some help with that?"

I snatched my hand away. "I don't need your help."

"What's going on out here?" The door flung open and my mom came out in the hallway.

"Uh, I was trying to get in the room," I said as I stumbled back a little.

"Girl, you are so embarrassing me, get your drunk behind in here now," my mom hissed. Then in a much nicer tone she said, "Hayden, come in please."

"Wasn't she just leaving?"

I was so confused when my mom went over to the girl

and just started explaining my behavior, like she needed to apologize to some college girl about how I was acting. My mom really needed to apologize to me for never giving me any of her time. "Come here, I want to introduce you guys. Malloy, this is one of my sorors from your school, Western Smith College," my mom said.

"See, I thought I knew you," the girl smiled. "I'm Hayden Grant. I'm going to be a junior at Western Smith College. I didn't know this was your mom."

"Yeah, sure you didn't know this was my mom," I said in a sarcastic tone.

"Lord, you don't have to be rude," my mom snapped.

"Then don't force me to talk to someone that I don't want to and don't try to apologize for me. I have a right to be angry, okay Mom? I don't want to embarrass you anymore, so please get this girl out of my face. I don't care what school she goes to. Unlike both of you, I don't think Beta Gamma Pi is God's gift to the world."

"Hayden, I am so sorry about this. Let's just keep this between us. My daughter doesn't usually drink. She'll be back to normal when you guys get back to school. Let's just say, I do look forward to working more closely with your chapter, particularly when she makes line."

"Yes ma'am," Hayden said, really getting on my nerves.

She could not get out of the suite fast enough for me. Of course, my mom looked at me like she was disappointed. Shucks, *I* was the one that was rightfully upset. The alcohol just allowed me to finally say how I felt.

"Mom, don't go making no promises to that girl about me being on line. I'm in school to get an education, not pledge. Plus, their last line was crazy. They haze up there.

You want me to have something to do with that? You're
the National President, you're supposed to be against any
form of hazing. I'm telling you it was all around school
that they put a girl from the last line in the hospital. One
of them will be dead soon."

She looked at me and rolled her eyes. I believed what I
was saying. Some of those girls would do anything to
wear the Greek letters. Not me.

"Sweetheart, if you're a part of the line they won't do
anything like that. I know you're tough. I don't have to
worry about anybody trying to do something you don't
want. Just promise me that you will at least consider
pledging. I've always wanted this for you, Malloy. Being
a part of this sisterhood can be so fulfilling. You don't
even have a best friend, for crying out loud."

"Yeah, for crying out loud, one of your biggest dreams
for me is to be in a sorority, not to fall in love with a man
and stay married forever, graduate from college with
honors and get a great job. Instead, you pray your child
gets into your sorority. I might have had a couple of
drinks, but it's clear to me that the thing you want for me
isn't what's best for me, it's what you want." I plopped
down on the couch, picked up the remote, turned on the
television and put the volume on high. "Don't hold your
breath on me becoming a Beta. Sweet dreams, Mommy."

She went into her part of the suite and slammed the
door. I knew I had disappointed her. However, as much
as she had disappointed me in my life, we weren't anywhere close to being even.